MURDER AT THE SPA

A Cedar Bay Cozy Mystery - Book 21

BY

DIANNE HARMAN

Published by: Dianne Harman
www.dianneharman.com

Interior, cover design and website by
Vivek Rajan

ISBN: 9798726556529

CONTENTS

ACKNOWLEDGMENTS

More and more we're reading about people who have found relatives they never knew they had through DNA tests, which in today's world, have become quite common. That, in addition to people researching their family trees through user-friendly internet sites, have caused some people to be very happy, and others not so much.

My daughter was recently researching our family tree, and in the course of the search, discovered that the man I had always been told was my great-grandfather was, in fact, not. It appears that my grandfather had been adopted by him. Interesting to have a part of your family history changed in an instant!

And I'm sure some of you know or have read about people who have put children up for adoption for one reason or another, and now, some of those children have been able to locate their biological parents using some form of DNA test. To say that lives have been upturned in many of these instances would be an understatement.

For those of you who have shared your stories with me, thank you!

To Vivek, Connie, and all the others who I depend on for each and every one of my books, thank you!

And to Tom, who painstakingly finds the glitches in my work, and lovingly, well, most of the time, points them out, thank you!

Win FREE Paperbacks every week!

Go to www.dianneharman.com/freepaperback.html and get your FREE copies of Dianne's books and favorite recipes immediately by signing up for her newsletter.

Once you've signed up for her newsletter you're eligible to win three paperbacks. One lucky winner is picked every week. Hurry before the offer ends!

CHAPTER ONE

"Doc, good to see you, as usual, and Liz, this is a pleasant surprise. You never come in here with Doc for lunch. I rather doubt that Kelly's Koffee Shop could survive without him," Kelly, the owner of the coffee shop said with a grin.

"Now Kelly, make nice," Doc said. "It's true I've been coming in here for lunch every day with the exception of the weekends, which amounts to about six years now, but consider it the ultimate compliment. There's nowhere else I'd rather go for lunch."

"Careful, Doc, remember your wife is with you, and she makes your lunch on the weekends. You may want to rethink that statement," Liz said in a teasing voice.

Doc held up his hands in mock surrender. "Let me rephrase that statement. When I go out to lunch during the week when I'm at work, I thoroughly enjoy coming to Kelly's Koffee Shop. However, when I'm at home on the weekends, I look forward to spending lunchtime there with my lovely wife."

He smiled at Liz. "Was that better?"

"Yes, you're forgiven," Liz said. "I see Roxie motioning to us. I think she's holding your booth for you."

"In that case, let's go. I probably wouldn't be able to enjoy my lunch if I had to eat at some other booth," Doc said.

Kelly walked into the kitchen to check with her cook, Charlie, and see if there was anything he needed.

"I'm good, Kelly. See that Doc and his wife are here. Let's just hope there aren't any physical or emotional emergencies in Cedar Bay during the next hour," Charlie said with a grin.

"Good point. With him being the only doctor in town, and her being the only psychologist, that could be a problem. "Thank heavens their medical building is just a few blocks away. They could be there in a couple of minutes."

Kelly picked up a couple of orders on the counter and said, "We're just starting the lunch rush, so don't be shy if you need some help."

"Kelly, I've been doing this for about ten years now for you. Tell me something. Have I ever asked for your help?" Charlie asked, keeping his head down while he concentrated on what he was cooking.

"Now that I think about it, Charlie, can't say that you have."

Kelly took the two orders she'd picked up and delivered

them to the table next to Doc and Liz. When she started to walk away, she heard Liz say, "Kelly, if you have a little time while we're here, I'd like to talk to you. Nothing urgent."

Kelly turned towards Liz and said, "Now's about as good of a time as any. It'll start picking up in a few minutes, and Roxie will give serious thought to quitting if she sees me sitting at a table while she's hustling around."

Kelly scooted into the booth across from Doc and Liz and said, "What's up?"

"I've got a proposition for you," Liz said.

"That sounds intriguing. What do you have in mind?" Kelly asked.

Liz looked over at Doc, who nodded, and she said, "Doc thinks I need a vacation. I've really been under the gun lately with some emotionally-draining clients. He suggested that I ask you to join me at a spa in the Willamette Valley. As you probably know, that area of Oregon is quite beautiful and, of course, is famous for the quality of wines that are produced there. Doc's even said he'll pay for everything."

"Wow, this comes out of the blue," Kelly said as she sat back in the booth.

"Kelly, there's a little more to it than that," Doc said. "That was just a bit of a teaser. Liz needs your help. You see, when she was young and had just started graduate school, she became pregnant. After she gave birth to a healthy baby girl, she placed the child for adoption with a couple her uncle, who was an attorney, knew." Doc turned and looked at Liz with a worried look on his face.

"It's okay, Doc," Liz said, putting her hand on his arm. "I can talk about it. Don't worry about me."

Liz turned towards Kelly and said, "I came from a small town and things like that were simply not allowed in that day and age, and particularly since my parents were very strait-laced religious people. They've since passed on, but that was the climate in which I grew up. Because of that experience and the whole tenor of the town, I've never been back, but now I think I have to."

"I'm old enough to remember that time," Kelly said, "and your story was a very common one back then."

"It certainly was. My daughter's adoptive family and I have remained in contact over the years. By our agreement, my daughter and I have never met, in fact I don't know if she even knows my name or how to get in touch with me."

"This is all very interesting, Liz," Kelly said, "but I fail to see what I have to do with any of this."

"She's getting there, Kelly. Just be patient," Doc said.

Liz took a deep breath. "The people who adopted my daughter became very wealthy. One of those fluke things. He bought a lottery ticket and won millions. They took the money and purchased a five-star resort with a spa and vineyard in the wine country area of the Willamette Valley, not too far from the town where I grew up."

"So is that where we'll be going? Won't that feel kind of awkward?" Kelly asked.

"Normally, I would have said yes to your question, and I would never have gone back to that town, however, something has come up," Liz said.

"I'm getting the feeling that the other shoe is about to drop. Would I be right?"

"Yes, and it concerns a situation involving my daughter."

"How old is your daughter and where is she?" Kelly asked.

Liz sighed deeply and said, "She's twenty-three, and at the moment she's in jail."

"I see. I assume her parents contacted you."

"Yes, they wondered if there was anything I could do to help," Liz said.

"Please don't tell me that you told them you had a friend who had been involved in solving a lot of criminal cases."

"No, I didn't," Liz said, looking over at Doc.

"Liz didn't, but I did," Doc said. "Liz had put the phone on speakerphone, and I answered for her, because she was momentarily overwhelmed. I told them about you, and said that you might be able to help."

"Swell. And?"

They were interrupted by Roxie who was bringing their lunch to them. "Doc, Liz, didn't even bother to bring you the menu, because I knew you'd want the special of the day, Charlie's chicken fajitas, and his apple pie. I've already had both, and speaking from experience, best thing on the menu today."

"Thanks, Roxie," Doc said. "You've never led me astray yet. Looking forward to this."

"Liz, Doc, I can see Randi waving to me," Kelly said. "Looks like there's a call I better take. I'll be right back."

A few minutes later Kelly returned to the booth where Liz and Doc were sitting, wearing a wide grin. "That was Cash. He and Kendra just got back from the doctor in Portland, and the baby is a boy. I'm going to have a grandson, woo-hoo! This is just perfect. I have two granddaughters, and now I'll have a grandson. Mike will probably get him a gun as a welcome to the world gift when he's born."

"I wouldn't expect anything less from a sheriff, and I'm sure you wouldn't either," Doc said. "Congrats to the family."

"Thanks, now let's get back to what we were talking about. Why is your daughter in jail?" Kelly asked.

"Murder," Liz said, a tear rolling down her cheek.

"Oh no!" Kelly said. "That's awful. Tell me everything you know."

Liz looked at Doc and he said, "We don't know much at all. Kelly, we hate to do this to you, but Liz really needs your help, and I mean like right now. I took the liberty of calling Mike and telling him about it. He thinks you and Liz should leave immediately and go there. He said he'd take care of everything at home, and he knew Roxie could handle things here."

"You're kidding. This is completely out of the blue. I'd need to pack, and I guess Mike is right, he can handle the house, and Roxie can take care of the coffee shop. But Doc, I'll be completely out of my element there. At least around here I know people, and I think that's pretty much why I've been successful in solving a couple of unfortunate murder cases."

"No, Kelly, you have a talent for this type of thing, and very few people do. Anyway, Mike said time is of the essence in a case like this. I think his exact words were, 'You don't have the luxury of taking your time with something like this.'"

"But Liz, what about your practice?" Kelly asked. "You'll have to cancel your patients."

"I already have Kelly. I'm free for the next week. It's a two-hour trip, and we can be there by late today. I'll drive. I can follow you to your house while you pack and then we can take off. My bag is in the car."

Kelly swallowed a couple of times and then she said, "Let me tell Roxie she'll have to take over for me for the next few days. I'll meet you in the parking lot."

CHAPTER TWO

"Liz, give me five minutes," Kelly said a few minutes later when she and Liz walked into her house. "I need to pack, and I want to call Mike."

Ten minutes later, when she walked back into the living room she said, "Okay, I'm ready. I called Mike, and he's glad I'm going. I'd like you to tell me everything you know on the way there."

Once they were on the highway on the way to the small town where the spa was located, Liz said, "Kelly, I really don't know all that much. The people who adopted my daughter are Amy and Chris Jannette. They named her Zoe.

"I transfer my psychology practice telephone number to my house when I leave the clinic after work, in case an emergency arises. I got a call last night about 10:00, and it was from Chris Jannette. He didn't have my personal number. As I mentioned earlier, they've sent me things from time to time over the years regarding Zoe, but they're sent by mail to my office address. That's the only way they have to get in touch with me."

"Probably smart to keep a step away from them like that," Kelly said.

"I thought it was, and then when I married Doc and told him about Zoe, he agreed. The Jannettes, Doc, and I all felt that it would be better for Zoe if there was no interaction between the two of us.

"Anyway, Chris was sobbing on the phone when he called and told me that Zoe had been arrested for murder. He said he didn't know the details, and he didn't know where to get help for her. He knew I was married to a doctor and thought since I was a psychologist, maybe I'd know some lawyers or people who might be able to help her."

"And I can see Doc taking the phone from you about that time, and offering my help," Kelly said.

"Sorry, Kelly, but yes, that's exactly what happened. He told them our local sheriff was one of our closest friends and that his wife had been responsible for solving a number of murder cases. He also told them that her son was a state Senator. Doc said he'd see if he could persuade you to help them."

"Chris was so appreciative," Liz said. "Doc told him he'd call him today and let him know if you'd be able to go there and see if you could do something to help. Doc called me while you were packing and told me he'd called Chris when he got back to the office after lunch.

"Chris is thrilled you're willing to help. They'll be at the hotel when we get there. Actually, I guess they have a house on the grounds and live there. We'll be staying in a suite at the hotel."

"Tell me what you know about the murder," Kelly said.

"Not much. Chris was so emotional he was having a hard time speaking coherently. What I did learn is that the murder victim was the spa manager. That's really all I know. Why Zoe was arrested I have not a clue. The last thing I heard was that she'd graduated from the University of Oregon, and that was two years ago."

"Do you know where she was arrested?"

"No. Really, Kelly, you now know as much as I do. I know she got a degree in Business Administration, and that's about it."

"Were the Jannettes planning on her helping them out in the business?"

"I don't know."

"How long have they owned the business?" Kelly asked.

"I think about fifteen years. They moved from the little town nearby to the resort, and as I said earlier, I only heard from them sporadically about Zoe."

"Liz, I know this is none of my business, but I need to know as much as possible about Zoe. What about her biological father? Was he from that area, and if so, do you know if he's still there?"

"He and I both were from there. When I got pregnant,

we were in graduate schools. Mine was psychology, his was law school. Neither one of us came from families with money, but we were both smart and ended up with scholarships to different universities. That's when I found out I was pregnant.

"I had the baby, and the Jannettes adopted her through my uncle who was an attorney. My parents never even knew I was pregnant and to my knowledge, my uncle kept his word and never told my parents."

"That must have been a horrible time for you."

"It was. Ryan, that's Zoe's biological father, was a year away from graduating, and it couldn't have come at a worse time. Both of us felt that giving the baby up for adoption would be best for the child, and for us as well."

"Did you stay in touch with the father?" Kelly asked.

"No. Ryan tried to get in touch with me a number of times, but there were too many unpleasant memories. I just couldn't bring myself to see him or talk to him. Eventually he quit calling."

"Does he know that the Jannettes adopted Zoe?"

"I don't know how he could. From what I heard from my parents, he finished law school and became a lawyer."

"And did he return to the small town you're from to practice law or go to some place like Portland or Salem?" Kelly asked.

"I don't know. My parents passed away, and there was no reason for me to go back there. Actually, the place held a lot of bad memories for me, and since I didn't want to ever set foot in the town again, I didn't keep up with anything or anybody."

Kelly's phone rang and she reached over and took it out of her purse. "Excuse me, Liz. My son, Cash, is on the phone." She pressed answer and said, "Congrats again, Cash. How's the new mother feeling?"

"She's fine, but that's not why I'm calling," Cash said. "Mike called me and told me that you're on your way to see if you can help Liz's daughter. I called the sheriff in that county and after applying a little pressure, was able to arrange for the best public defender in that area to meet with you and Liz when you get there."

"Thanks, Cash. I guess that's one of the benefits of being in the Oregon State Senate, although you haven't been there all that long. Is this the first time you've had to use a bit of political leverage?"

"Sure is, but figured if I can't help my mother and one of her closest friends, then all the work I had to do to get to the Senate wouldn't be worth it. Anyway, the public defender's name is Finn O'Conner. He'll have all the information about why she was arrested and everything that's known so far."

"Where should we meet him?"

"How about at the jail? How much longer until you'll be there?" Cash asked.

Kelly looked over at Liz who was shaking her head. "Wait a minute, Cash. Liz wants to say something to me."

She turned to Liz.

"Kelly, I will drive you to the jail so you can meet this man, but I'm not going in. And we should be there in about an hour."

"Why?"

"Because I don't want the first time Zoe and I see each other to take place in jail, and I rather doubt that she'd want her biological mother to see her there. I'll wait for you in the car."

"Are you sure?" Kelly asked. "It could be a while."

"Yes, I'm absolutely sure. Maybe when this whole thing is over, she and I can talk, but not under these circumstances."

"I respect that," Kelly said and then began to talk into her phone. "Cash, I'll be the only one meeting Finn. Tell him I'll be there in about an hour. If he's not there, I'll wait for him in the reception area, or whatever they have there that serves as one."

"Will do. And Mom, you're not going to like this, but Finn told me since she's been charged with murder, the judge in that jurisdiction will not allow her to get out of jail on bail. He has an absolute ironclad rule about that. Unfortunately, she's going to be a jail resident until you can determine that someone, other than Liz's daughter, committed the murder, and by the way, I have the utmost confidence in you that you will."

"Thanks, Cash. Hope I earn your confidence. Tell Finn I'm looking forward to meeting him."

"Will do, and keep me in the loop."

CHAPTER THREE

"This looks like the jail, Kelly," Liz said an hour later. "I'm going to park here in the shade. Take your time and do whatever you need to do. I just saw a man walk in the front door. I'll bet he's the public defender."

"What makes you say that? Could just be a visitor for someone who's in jail."

"Kelly, look at the size of this jail. I'd be surprised if it has more than six cells. Trust me, there are only small towns in this area, and other than the Hillside Resort that the Jannettes own, there's not much more. Sure, as you can see, there are a couple of businesses in this town, but no big box ones. Anyway, back to the lawyer, he's wearing a suit and carrying a briefcase."

"Point well taken. Liz, do you want me to say anything to Zoe for you? I don't know if the Jannettes have told her that we're coming up here, but I would imagine they have."

"No. Not yet. Just do what you have to do to get her out," Liz said as a tear started to run down her cheek.

I absolutely hate this, Kelly thought, *but I do understand her reasoning. Sometimes I wish I didn't see both sides of a story. Sure would make my life easier.*

Kelly opened the door of the jail and immediately found herself in a small room with a sheriff's deputy sitting at a desk and a man in a suit sitting in one of the two chairs along the back wall. As soon as she entered, the man stood up and took two steps over to her, his hand outstretched.

"You must be Kelly Reynolds. I'm Finn O'Conner." He turned to the deputy sheriff and said, "Is there a room where I can talk to Mrs. Reynolds privately?"

The deputy looked them both over and said, "Yeah, open that door," he said, pointing to one next to where Finn had been sitting. "You can go in there. It's quiet, and you can talk. Let me know if you need something from me."

Finn motioned for Kelly to follow him and opened the door to the small room. "Please, have a seat, and I'll fill you in on the little I know," he said.

Kelly sat down, and Finn sat at a small table across from her. He opened his briefcase and took out a file. "Mrs. Reynolds, I'm sorry to say I don't have much information for you on this case."

"Stop," Kelly said. "Please call me Kelly."

"And I'm Finn. Here's what I do know. Zoe Jannette was arrested yesterday evening around 9:00 p.m. at her home at the Hillside Resort for the murder of Tina Lindsay, the spa manager at the resort."

"Do you know why she was charged with murder?"

"According to the report, the cleaning lady, Maria Castro, was the one who found the decedent. She was finishing up for the evening, the last thing being for her to clean the room where the jacuzzi is located. When she went inside, she saw Tina Lindsay, presumably dead in the jacuzzi, with blood in the water. She called 911.

"The officers spent the next day interviewing people. The cleaning lady said she had seen Zoe Jannette walk out the door of the jacuzzi about a half hour before she went in to clean it and lock it up for the night. Along with that, several employees said earlier in the day they heard Tina and Zoe in an argument regarding records that Tina didn't want to turn over to her. Based on that, she was charged with murder."

"Doesn't that seem very convenient? Is that the full extent of the evidence?" Kelly asked.

"No. The assistant manager, Raquelle DuBois, had been working late at her office in the spa. The jacuzzi is attached to it. As she was walking to her car, she heard sirens entering the property. She was curious and followed the officers. They interviewed her and she said that she had taken a walk round the spa area to inspect everything before she left, and she had seen Zoe come out of the jacuzzi door about a half hour before Tina's body was discovered."

"When is Zoe's arraignment?" Kelly asked.

"Monday morning. The judge is attending a judicial conference today, so she couldn't be arraigned today."

"From what my son told me based on what you told him, I understand this judge doesn't grant bail in murder cases."

"That's correct. Judge Murphy is a real stickler. He's not a judge that I like to see on the bench when I'm defending a case, I'll tell you that," Finn said with a shrug of his shoulders. "And there's something else you should know that makes me uncomfortable."

"What's that?" Kelly asked.

"The sheriff of this county, Dirk Kuyper, doesn't really let the facts of the case interfere when he wants to make an arrest."

"What do you mean by that?"

"He's very ambitious and being sheriff is just a stepping stone to being the sheriff of a much more populated county or something. He's got a good reputation, and there's a good chance that he'll be able to accomplish that goal."

"Are you telling me that some other sheriff might not have arrested Zoe based on the meager evidence you've told me about?" Kelly asked.

"Yes, unfortunately Sheriff Kuyper feels the law is his to manipulate."

"Wow. That's going to make this doubly hard. Finn, I know we need to talk to Zoe, but what is your sense of the case at this point?"

"Something feels very off to me, Kelly. I haven't had a

chance to talk to Zoe yet. I figured as long as you were coming, I'd hold off, so she didn't have to tell her story twice. I understand that you're going to see if you can find out who the murderer is, so the case against Zoe can be dismissed. Quite frankly, I think you have your work cut out for you."

"I think you're right. I'm hoping Zoe might have some thoughts on who did it and, if so, why she was framed. However, I do need to tell you something before we talk to her."

"What's that?" Finn asked.

Kelly spent the next few minutes explaining the circumstances of her being involved in the case and Zoe's and Liz's relationship. "I was thinking on the way here that the best way to introduce me is to say that you had talked briefly with the family, and they'd asked if you knew any private investigators. I thought you could say that you did, and you contacted me. Depending on how Liz wants to play this, we can tell Zoe the truth later, but I doubt if she needs anything more dumped on her right now."

"I agree. I'll simply introduce you as someone I use in cases like this. I doubt we'll have to elaborate. I'm sure Zoe's main focus right now is not going to be on who you are, but more on what you can do for her."

"Thanks for being so understanding, Finn. Let's go talk to Zoe."

CHAPTER FOUR

Raquelle DuBois drove into her driveway and clicked the garage door opener on her sun visor. After she parked her car in the garage, she took the groceries out of the trunk and walked into her kitchen. As she began putting the groceries away, she moved about the kitchen in an almost robot-style manner, because her mind was several miles away, at the Hillside Spa.

Over a year ago, Amy Jannette, one of the spa's owners, had told the spa manager, Tina Lindsay, that she wanted Tina to concentrate on actively promoting the spa. Tina had taken some courses in computer advertising, and Amy thought it would be a great way to increase the spa's traffic. She'd suggested to Tina that Raquelle, the assistant manager of the spa, could take over the bookkeeping, which would free up Tina for her new expanded duties.

It had seemed like a perfect solution to Amy, having remembered that Raquelle had majored in accounting in college. What Amy hadn't or couldn't have known was that Raquelle had been terminated by her prior employer for embezzling funds. Since she was having an affair with the owner who had discovered the embezzlement, the two of them entered into an informal agreement.

Raquelle wouldn't tell his wife about the affair if he agreed to give her a good employment recommendation and omit anything about the embezzlement. He'd kept his word, and she'd kept hers. The only loser was Amy Jannette, because Raquelle had been given an outstanding reference by her previous employer, which made Amy feel very comfortable about hiring her. She was sure Raquelle would be a good employee.

Prior to Raquelle taking over the bookkeeping, her main job had been to oversee the large spa staff. She was in charge of hiring and on occasion, having to fire employees. She had an assistant who handled all of the spa appointments. As the new bookkeeper, she was on the spa bank account and took care of the bank deposits and payments for supplies, employee's checks, and everything else that dealt with the financial aspects of the spa.

It had taken her a few months to figure out how she could skim money from the bank account, but since she was the only one now handling the books, it had been fairly easy. Particularly since Tina had been more than willing to look the other way, as long as she was paid a percentage of the money she skimmed from the bank account.

Amy had an employee at the hotel who handled the hotel's finances, which freed Amy from the day-to-day business and allowed her to concentrate on being wherever she was needed, so that both the spa and the hotel could remain successful. And they were enormously successful.

Being the only five-star resort with a spa in a wine region

known for its pinot noir was very advantageous. Plus, Amy and Chris had started bottling their own wine a few years earlier, and now had an active wine business along with a tasting room that was attached to the hotel.

There was another spa about ten miles from where the Hillside Spa was located, but because it wasn't part of a hotel complex, it had to rely on day use only customers. There was always talk that the owner was in meetings with one developer or another to build a hotel adjacent to the spa, but so far that's all it had been, talk.

Raquelle wasn't worried about the threat of competition from a new hotel. What she was concerned about was that Amy had recently told her that her daughter, Zoe, was being groomed to manage both the hotel and spa.

Amy had said that Zoe had spent a lot of time learning the bookkeeping system used at the hotel as well as various other aspects of the hotel business, and that sometime soon she wanted Zoe to focus her attention on the spa. As such, Amy had told Raquelle that when it came time for Zoe to learn about the financial aspects of the spa, she wanted Raquelle to help her learn about the bookkeeping system at the spa and give her full access to the books.

She'd also told Raquelle that it might be a good idea for Zoe to completely take over the bookkeeping for a couple of weeks, so she could see how it worked from start to finish.

Raquelle knew that anyone who was competent in bookkeeping would easily spot the discrepancies in the books, and at some point, Raquelle's embezzling would come to light.

Tina, the spa manager, was very resistant to Zoe coming in and having access to the books for the same reason that Raquelle was. It wouldn't take long for Zoe to figure out that Raquelle had been embezzling funds from the spa's bank account, and there was a good chance that Tina would be implicated, too.

Amy had told Raquelle she had planned to move Zoe over to the spa sometime in the next couple of weeks, but because she had too much on her plate at the moment, she'd moved the date to implement the change back a couple of weeks. Raquelle and Tina agreed that the short delay would give Raquelle time to make a duplicate set of books or take whatever steps were necessary in order to hide the evidence of the embezzlement from Zoe.

Raquelle had never wanted to spend her life working for someone else. The whole purpose of her embezzling money from employers had been to pad her personal bank account with the stolen funds, so she could retire to Mexico and enjoy the rest of her life relaxing in the sun. Just a few more months of embezzling funds would set her up for good. She'd have enough to buy a piece of property and live the good life in Mexico.

Her mother had been from Mexico, and Raquelle had learned Spanish from her at an early age. In fact, that was the way she and her mother had always communicated, in Spanish, until she'd passed away a few years ago. It was because of her that Raquel had fallen in love with Mexico. She and her mother had gone there several times a year to visit her mother's side of the family.

Raquelle knew she was very close to her dream of living in Mexico. She only needed a few more months, but now she was getting hit with this new wrinkle. If Zoe discovered the discrepancies in the books, not only would her dream be unrealized, there was a good chance that instead of spending her days on the beach in Mexico, she'd be spending them in an orange jumpsuit in a prison yard.

As she was putting away the groceries the thought occurred to her that if she could get rid of both Tina and Zoe, her problems would be over. Tina already knew she was embezzling funds from the spa's bank account and Zoe would soon discover the crime, so if they were both gone, she'd be in the clear.

An idea came to her, and although she initially rejected it, the more she thought about it, the more sense it made. If the two of them weren't around, it would buy her time, and she'd be long gone when the bookkeeping discrepancies were discovered at some later time.

If she murdered Tina and framed Zoe for the crime, they'd both be gone. Tina would be deceased and Zoe would be in the state penitentiary. Problem solved. Hello, Mexico, here I come. Plus, she imagined the Jannette family would be in mourning over Zoe's incarceration. And if Tina was dead, who better to take over the spa manager's job than Raquelle?

The Jannette family would just be happy that someone was willing to do it, because they'd be too grief-stricken to take care of it themselves. That would provide her with an even bigger opportunity to dip into the spa's bank account.

Then another thought occurred to her. Since she'd been having an affair with Tina's husband, Brett, for the last few months, and he'd told her many times how he wished he could get divorced and he and Raquelle could be together, this could work. She knew Brett was as amoral as she was, and she thought there was a good chance he might be interested in going to Mexico with her.

As Raquelle finished putting the groceries away, her mind was working at warp speed. She walked into her office and sat down, making notes. When she was finished, she picked up the phone, pressed in Brett's numbers and said, "Brett, I think I have a solution to all of our problems."

CHAPTER FIVE

"Thanks for coming. Hope that solves your problem," Brett Lindsay said to the couple who were walking out of his hardware store. He looked around, once again wondering how he'd let himself be talked into taking over the family business when his father had become ill. He hated anything to do with hardware, yet here he was. Stuck.

His parents had passed away several years ago, and he could have sold the store, but he had nowhere else to go, and there was also the fact that buyers for a hardware store in Rolling Hills Crossing would be few and far between, if they even existed. Rolling Hills Crossing was a small town, but like many small towns, there were certain stores that were essential to it, and Lindsay Hardware was one of them.

There were a number of wineries in the area who depended on Lindsay Hardware when they had a problem with equipment, which was why his hardware store was a little different than most. Actually, with the scarce population in the area, most of his business came from the wineries. When they needed a part, they needed it now.

Time was money to them, and since most of them operated on a very slim profit margin, having production down for even a couple of hours was critical, so rather than stock all the things traditionally needed for homeowners, his hardware inventory was heavy on items the wineries would need.

Brett sat down and opened a can of beer. There weren't any customers in the store, and if today was like most other days, he'd be lucky if he had more than two or three the rest of the day. Then again, maybe he'd get lucky and one of the wineries would have a major breakdown. That could make his month.

As he took a swig of the cold beer, he thought about how he'd ever ended up here. He'd been the star quarterback in high school, in love with the head cheerleader. Great things were expected of Brett Lindsay. Everyone in the small town was sure he'd get a full scholarship to the University of Oregon, and some of the more optimistic townspeople even had hopes that he'd go on to win the Heisman Trophy.

But none of those things happened because of his last high school game. In the last minute of the game, he'd thrown a pass and then been tackled by the two hundred fifty pound defensive end of the opposing team. The referee threw a flag because of the illegal tackle, but it was too late. The damage had been done. Brett's leg had been shattered in several places, and he'd never play football again.

All of Brett's dreams ended on the football field that

night. As he was put in an ambulance to be taken to the county hospital, he knew he'd never go to the University of Oregon or play football again. His grades weren't good enough to get into the university, and even if they had been, his parents couldn't afford it.

The hardware store just barely paid their bills as it was, and they lived in the same house his grandparents and great-grandparents had lived in. At least it was free and clear.

He'd been sure Tina would break up with him, but she hadn't, she'd stayed with him. He'd been surprised, but then he thought that she really didn't have anything else going on in her life besides him. Her parents were unable to send her to college and having no skills, she'd started working at the Hillside Spa as a towel girl.

Over the years she'd studied computer science at a local junior college, and when the Jannettes had bought the spa, she'd continued to work there. The woman who had been the spa manager for a number of years decided to retire, and Tina had stepped into the position.

She and Brett had gotten married when they'd graduated from high school because it seemed like the thing to do. In hindsight, it was about the only thing to do. Their lives had settled into a pattern, Tina worked at the spa, and Brett worked at the hardware store, eventually taking it over when his father became ill, and then died.

Brett had never asked Tina if she was happy or had dreams of a better life, but he did. He dreamed of a life where he wouldn't have to go into the hardware store every day, hoping that one of the wineries had had an equipment failure during the night.

He dreamed of a life where he didn't have to go to church with his wife's family every Sunday and then have dinner at their home with them. It wasn't that he disliked them, it was just that after so many years, he found them boring. It seemed like every week they had the same conversation. At times Brett felt like he was suffocating. It was as if he'd dug himself into a huge hole, and he couldn't crawl out of it.

Sure, he had passing thoughts of coming into money and traveling to exotic places. Dreams of women who were alluring and didn't look at him like he was a failure. He knew Tina thought he was. He could tell it in her eyes when he caught her looking at him, but she always tried to hide it. Brett wanted an out, an escape from his boring dead-end life.

Then one day a few months ago he'd gone to the spa to pick up his checkbook from Tina, and he'd met Raquelle DuBois. That was the day he felt like life had been breathed back into him. He didn't really know how dead he'd been until then.

When he met Raquelle it was as if everything changed in Brett's life. The hills were greener. The sun shone brighter. The television sitcoms were funnier, and life was worth living again. Brett had been cautious, not wanting to raise any alarms in Tina, but within a month, Raquelle and Brett had become lovers.

It required a great deal of creativity on their part not to be seen together at all, because the people of Rolling Hills Crossing didn't have much else to do for entertainment other than gossip.

Brett didn't quite know what to do with his new feelings. He really had never experienced anything like this in his life. He wanted to leave Rolling Hills Crossing and start a new life with Raquelle, but he knew he didn't have the funds to do it.

They'd talked about it a couple of times, and Raquelle had always told him to be patient, that she had a plan, but she'd never confided in him exactly what that plan was. He looked at his watch and saw that he still had two more hours to stay at the store until he could turn over the open sign to closed.

He turned on the little television he kept under the counter, opened a beer, and began to watch a movie. A little after 7:00 the phone rang, and he answered it. It was Raquelle.

"Brett, I think I have a solution to our problems. I know the store is open late tonight, and I need a couple of door stoppers. I think the puppy I got a few months ago has eaten them. I thought we could talk for a while, and if anyone comes in, you're just selling me some merchandise."

When Raquelle left the hardware store later that evening, Brett knew his problems had been solved. It was going to take a little while, but Raquelle's plan would work, and if for some reason it didn't, he could probably find a way to get his hands on the money that Tina, unbeknownst to Brett, had been collecting from Raquelle.

CHAPTER SIX

Cody Merritt walked out of the Merritt Spa and locked the door behind him. He took a deep breath, trying to get rid of the frustration he felt. Once again, talks with another hotel developer had fallen apart, and he wasn't sure what he was going to do.

He turned around and looked at his spa with fresh eyes, eyes that a prospective developer would use. The spa, with its Mediterranean architecture, had twelve treatment rooms built in a horseshoe formation around a fountain area with lush potted plants. The rooms all opened out to the area and the fountain sounds were soothing to the guests.

Cody knew his spa could be more successful than the Hillside Spa if only he could get a developer to come in and build a hotel adjacent to it. When he'd decided to build the spa, he'd borrowed heavily against the land he'd inherited from his parents, fertile land that would easily grow the pinot noir grapes for which the region was so well-known.

He'd had to make a choice when he'd inherited the land. Plant grapes or build a spa. Cody was in far too much of a hurry to wait the approximate five years it took for the grapevines to grow and reach maturity, so he'd opted for the spa. He was certain that a developer would jump at the chance to build a hotel in the wine country.

Cody had been very, very wrong. The scenery was beautiful, but the country was in a mini-recession and the last thing any developer wanted to do was commit to building a multimillion dollar building in a down economy. Plus, the hotel would be in direct competition with the Hillside Hotel and Spa, which was a five-star hotel with an excellent reputation.

Cody had to rely on people in the nearby towns and occasional guests from the Hillside Spa as his customers. Unfortunately, the towns were small, and other than the sporadic wealthy vintners, there wasn't a lot of disposable income in the community that could be used by the local residents for going to a spa for a treatment.

In addition to the guests, it was a challenge to find competent spa help in the remote area. He'd been able to find some, but he'd also had to hire several people who also worked part-time at the Hillside Spa, which galled him to no end.

Quite frankly Cody wasn't sure what he was going to do. He was breaking even on the spa and lived on the income that he got from the farmers he rented his land to. He'd had several requests from wine growers to grow grapes on his property, but the leases they'd insisted on, ten-year leases, would tie up the land and prevent him from ever building a hotel.

He knew the Jannettes and most of the staff at their spa.

As a matter of fact, he'd gone to school with Tina and Brett Lindsay. Cody was surprised when Tina had been named as the spa manager, because he'd never thought she was all that bright.

Cody felt that the bright one in the spa was Raquelle DuBois, but when she'd moved to the area and applied for a job with him, he had an instant negative reaction to her. It was completely unfounded, but he usually acted on his feelings, and over the years, he'd come to rely on them. When he started hearing from some Hillside Spa employees that they were having problems with their paychecks, he was glad he had.

He kept thinking of how he could make this work, how his spa could become successful. One thing he considered was going to the Jannettes and talk to them about having the Merritt Spa become the second location of the Hillside Spa and rename it something like Hillside Spa No. 2.

He thought if he could get them to agree to that, he'd have a built-in clientele, referrals from the Hillside Spa. He'd give them a percentage of whatever the guests spent at his spa and everybody would win. Plus, it would give the guests at the Hillside Hotel an alternative venue for their treatments.

Cody had made an appointment with Amy, who seemed to be the one handling the hotel and spa, while her husband, Chris handled everything having to do with their wine and tasting room. He'd presented his idea to her, and she said she'd think about it and that she needed to run it by her husband.

She called a few days later and told Cody that she and

Chris had decided to just continue to operate the spa as it was presently, and she'd wished him good luck.

Cody began to feel like he was between a rock and a hard place. He still had a couple of real estate development companies who were showing an interest in the property. They'd told him they might be interested in developing something in a few years, but right now was not a good time for them.

He began to think if he could do something to create a scandal at the Hillside Spa, something that would be a reason people wouldn't want to go there, their spa business would spill over to his spa. And that might be enough to get him through the next couple of years, at least until the hotel was built on his land. But now the question was what.

He knew it would have to be something big. Something that would scare people away from the spa. He thought of a fire, but then decided that could be a problem, because if there was a fire at the spa, a spark or flame could ignite the hotel, and he needed the hotel guests. Plus, the county fire department was quite a ways from the Hillside property and there was a good chance it would burn to the ground before it could be put out.

Then another thought occurred to him. What if the manager of the spa was murdered? He'd never really liked Tina Lindsay, anyway. Ever since she'd been the head cheerleader in high school and going with the star quarterback, she lorded it over everyone in their small school. That had been a long time ago, but teenage hurts have a way of staying with people. And that one had stayed with Cody for a long, long time.

The more he thought about it, the more the idea appealed to him. Who'd want to go to a spa where a murder had occurred? And then he thought what if it occurred in the jacuzzi? Jacuzzis were a hugely popular part of spas, and if a murder occurred in one, that sure would stop a lot people from wanting to go to the spa. It would ruin their whole experience.

And the alternative? Easy. The alternative would be to go to the Merritt Spa. Plus, he'd get revenge on Tina Lindsay for making him feel like such a nerd. Which was probably why he still felt like one.

And the best part of it was that everyone knew Tina took a soak in the jacuzzi after the spa closed at 8:00 p.m. before she headed home at night. She said it relaxed her. It really would be easy, because so few people were around at that time of night. And why would anyone consider Cody to be a suspect when everyone knew Tina's spa schedule?

Cody smiled, a real smile, for the first time in a long time and decided to treat himself to that expensive bottle of pinot noir he'd been saving for a special occasion. Finding a solution to solve this problem was indeed a special occasion.

CHAPTER SEVEN

"I hope you enjoy this pinot noir," Tiffany Ruiz said. "It's grown here at the Hillside property, and has received a number of awards. It's a medium-dry red wine that is typically fruit forward."

"What does fruit forward mean? I've not heard that term before," the man in the sport coat asked as he swirled the wine in the glass of wine Tiffany had poured for him.

Obviously not from around here wearing a sport coat. I'd put him from Portland. He's probably staying at the hotel and tasting wines at the different tasting rooms in the valley, Tiffany thought.

"We use that term to describe a style of wine where the fruit flavors are dominant. I believe you'll be able to pick up the flavors of dark cherries, red currant, and berries. Sometimes the term is used to describe a wine that is out of balance or lacking complexity. It can also refer to wines that are cheap and one-dimensional, but that's obviously not the case here, as you'll see when you taste it."

The man took several sips of it and then said, "I'd like a

case of this. Please give me some others that you recommend."

"I'll be happy to, sir," Tiffany said.

An hour later he handed her his credit card to complete the $638.00 transaction. Ricky and Jeff, the two young men who worked in the Hillside Winery Tasting Room carried the cases of wine that he purchased to his car.

Tiffany thought about how easy it had been to get him to buy the wines. Kind of like shooting fish in a barrel. She knew she had a natural gift for getting people to buy wine, but that wasn't what she wanted to do.

She'd been hired by Amy a couple of years earlier to work at the spa. Amy told her she wanted Tiffany to learn several of the jobs at the spa and then she would put her in the position of assistant spa manager, only that hadn't happened.

Tiffany had worked at the spa for a week when she'd gotten a call from Amy to meet her in the tasting room. Rosie, the woman who had worked there since it had opened, had a family emergency. Her daughter had been diagnosed with cancer, and Rosie had quit, with no notice, to fly to Kansas City to take care of her grandchildren.

Amy had told her she needed Tiffany to start working there immediately and that they would be hiring a replacement for Rosie as soon as they could, so she could return to the spa. Fortunately, or unfortunately, Tiffany was a self-taught wine person, and she soon made a lie of the "Peter Principle." The real Peter Principle was, "the idea that people are promoted until they reach the level at which they are no longer competent."

Tiffany had been promoted, if one wanted to call being a gofer in the spa to becoming a wine teacher, being promoted. However, instead of reaching her level of incompetence, she had reached such a level of competence that Chris was really torn about replacing Rosie with anyone other than Tiffany.

Tiffany had brought it up to Amy a number of times, that she wanted to return to the spa and work there, but Amy had always told Tiffany that she'd do it down the road. For now, she wanted to continue with Tiffany working in the wine tasting room because she was so good at it.

But that wasn't what Tiffany wanted. Tiffany had always wanted to be the manager of a spa. Even as a young girl, she'd spend all her babysitting money on magazines about spas. She knew what was popular and what wasn't. She'd become an expert on which products really worked and which products were a waste of money.

She wanted to be the manager of the Hillside Spa. It was a very prestigious spa, and she knew if she could make a go of working in the wine tasting room when she hated it, she'd be fabulous if she could work at what she really wanted to do.

Tiffany had talked a number of times with Tina about the spa and what she'd read about hot new treatments and products. She'd ask Tina to hire her in some capacity, but Tina always had one excuse or another, even when the assistant manager's job had been open, which Tiffany had applied for. But Tina told her she'd hired someone with more experience, although Tiffany later found out that Raquelle had no spa experience.

Tiffany had more experience working just one week at the Hillside Spa before she was transferred to the wine tasting room than Raquelle did. Tiffany had come to believe that for some reason, Tina did not want her to work at the spa. She had no idea why Tina was so opposed to her being there, other than she might be threatened by Tiffany's knowledge.

The more Tiffany thought about it the more she was convinced that Tina was sabotaging her attempts to work at the spa. She was probably afraid that Tiffany could take over her job, and Tiffany was sure she could do a much better job than Tina had done.

It seemed to Tiffany that Tina was stuck in a rut. She hadn't seen any real innovations at the spa since she'd started working there. It seemed to her that Tina's thinking was similar to the old adage, "If it ain't broke, don't fix it."

And Tiffany grudgingly had to admit there was probably some truth in that. Certainly, the spa was busy year round, actually, most days it was pretty much at full capacity. But she kept thinking about the potential. If she was the manager, she'd bring in the newest spa techniques and equipment.

The spa would become known as THE spa to go to in the Pacific Northwest. Tiffany was sure she could get it to be one of the ten best spas in the United States like Mii

Amo in Sedona, Arizona. Then the hotel traffic would increase as well as the wine sales. It seemed like a win-win situation to her, but how to implement it? How to get rid of Tina?

Tiffany didn't think Tina was going anywhere soon. Her husband owned that little hardware store in Rolling Hills Crossing that barely made enough money to keep it open. She knew they needed Tina's income from the spa, so she was sure Tina would keep on working for years, and by then Tiffany might be too old to even be considered for the position.

Finally she arrived at a defining moment when she realized she had no choice. She'd never been a violent person or done anything illegal or that could even be construed as a crime, but she really had been left with no choice. Tina had to go. Now it was just a matter of figuring out how.

CHAPTER EIGHT

Finn and Kelly stepped back into the small reception room and told the deputy that they were there to see Zoe Jannette. Finn told him that he was the public defender in the case.

The deputy asked them to follow him and opened the door to a small room where there were four chairs and a small table. The deputy asked if they would like him to remain in the room while they talked to Zoe, and Finn said no.

They sat down and a few minutes later the deputy opened the door and a young woman with flaming red hair walked in. Her eyes were red-rimmed, indicating that she'd been crying. She sat down and said, "This is all new to me. I have no idea what to do or say."

"Zoe, I'm Finn O'Conner, and I'll be representing you as your attorney in this case. I'm the Hill County Public Defender. This is my associate that I use on cases, Kelly Reynolds. She's very good at solving crimes. Let's start by you telling us how you came to be arrested."

"Alright. My parents and I found out night before last that Tina Lindsay had been murdered in the jacuzzi at the spa my parents own, the Hillside Spa. Yesterday the sheriff talked to several people at the spa, as well as to me and my parents.

"Last night the sheriff came to my home on the hotel property and arrested me for the murder of Tina Lindsay," Zoe said as she started to cry.

"Alright. Let's back up. When the sheriff talked to you yesterday, what did you tell him? What specifically did he ask you?" Finn asked.

"He wanted to know where I had been at the time of the murder, which he said was somewhere between 8:00 and 9:00. I told him I'd taken a walk with my dog about 8:00 and had gone around the spa and jacuzzi and then Niko and I walked back to my home. I have a small house on the property."

"What did you do then?"

"I fixed dinner. I remember I had music playing and was thinking how much I was enjoying the dinner with the music when I heard something. Now I know it was sirens, but I had the music volume turned up quite a ways, so it took me a few minutes to realize that's what I was hearing. The sound of sirens was so foreign to our resort that it didn't register with me initially.

"I walked out of my house and saw an ambulance and several sheriff's cars. A few minutes later a white van with the words, Hill County Coroner, pulled up. I saw my parents talking to the sheriff and the others and then I saw a body being loaded into the coroner's van.

"I walked over to where my parents were, and they told me that someone had murdered Tina Lindsay in the jacuzzi and that the sheriff and his deputies would be talking to everyone who worked at the spa the next day. I understand that the person who found Tina, Maria Castro, was really shook up, but she gave a statement and they allowed her to leave. Most of the spa employees were already gone for the day, as it was getting late, and shortly thereafter, the remaining people left."

"What did your parents think?" Finn asked.

"Naturally, they were very concerned that something like that had happened on their property. Tina had been with the spa for some time, so of course they were terribly upset that she'd been murdered, and they couldn't understand why."

"Alright, Zoe. On the night of the murder, did you talk to the sheriff or any of his deputies?"

"No, when they left, my parents went to their house, and I went back to mine."

"Okay, tell me about the next day."

"The spa opens at 8:00 in the morning. The sheriff and one of his deputies were there. I was there when they came, along with the people who were scheduled to work that day. Everyone was very upset about what had happened to Tina, and the yellow crime scene tape on the jacuzzi's door didn't help. We all felt like we were in a murder scene on some television show.

"Did the sheriff and his deputy begin to take statements from the people associated with the spa?"

"Yes. They graciously waited until the employees were on break so they wouldn't upset the guests who had appointments scheduled. I think they finished with them around noon. Then they left."

"When were you arrested?"

"Yesterday evening. I was working late and had just left the spa to walk over to my house to let Nico out. That's when I saw the sheriff and a couple of deputies drive into the spa parking lot. One of his men walked over to me and told me I was under arrest for the murder of Tina Lindsay. They told me two employees had seen me leaving the jacuzzi around the time of her murder. Additionally, they said several employees had heard an argument between Tina and me that occurred earlier on the day she was murdered."

"Alright. You mentioned you'd taken your dog for a walk about the time of the murder. Since two employees saw you leaving the jacuzzi about that time, were you walking your dog with a leash or was he off-leash?" Finn asked.

"Since the property was fenced, he was off-leash. Nico's a Belgian Malinois and previously belonged to a friend of mine. Her husband was a police officer in the K-9 unit and was killed in a drug investigation. After his death, she decided to return to her parents' home in Georgia and asked if I'd take Nico.

"He'd been expertly trained by the police, so I never

have him on a leash. He likes to sniff the trees in the area, so he probably wasn't walking next to me when they saw him. Quite frankly, I don't remember," Zoe said.

"Okay, tell me about the argument you had with Tina."

"I don't know which employees heard the argument, but her office is located in the middle of the treatment rooms, so raised voices certainly could easily be heard. My parents have been grooming me to take over a lot of the day-to-day business operations of the resort for them. They're getting older and don't want to work quite as hard as they have been to make Hillside such a success. They want to travel, except they feel like they're tied to the resort and can't get away.

"I've been working with the manager of the hotel, learning all the ins-and-outs, as well as the bookkeeping," Zoe said. "I've also done the same with the wine, although my dad still wants to oversee it, because it's kind of his baby.

"Which leaves the spa as the last thing for you to learn about," Kelly surmised.

"Yes. I went into Tina's office to ask her to give me a firm date and time when I could start looking at the records. I wanted to see all of the data regarding treatment appointments for guests, product purchases and sales, information on the people we hire as facialists, massage therapists, etc. And I also wanted full access to all the bookkeeping."

"Would that require a lot of work from her to get it ready for you to look at?" Finn asked.

"Yes, some, but it wouldn't take much time to assemble and certainly wouldn't be enough to divert her attention from the other aspects of her job duties. Anyway, she got angry and said this was the third time I'd asked her, which it was, and to stop nagging her. She told me she'd get to it in the next few weeks."

"And I take it that didn't go over well with you," Kelly said.

"No, it didn't. I've been reminded a number of times that I have a typical redhead's temper. And it's probably true. I lost my temper and told her I wanted access the next day, and if she didn't have the information and records I needed from her by then, I'd make sure that she would soon be looking for another job."

"And your voices were raised?" Finn asked.

"Yes, we both were almost yelling. Then she said I was nothing but a spoiled brat who had never had an honest job in my life, and that if it wasn't for my parents, I'd be on welfare."

"I imagine that didn't make you very happy," Finn said drily.

"No, it infuriated me. I told her to make sure the data was ready for me by 9:00 a.m. the next morning, then I slammed the door and left," Zoe said.

"And a couple of employees heard it. Did she use your name specifically during the argument?" Kelly asked.

"Yes."

"So there was no doubt in the minds of the employees that you were the one having an argument with her?" Kelly asked.

"I'm sure they knew it was me, but I didn't kill her. She wasn't my favorite person, but I wasn't the one who did it."

"I think the next thing we need to do, Zoe, is for you to try and come up with the names of people who might be considered possible suspects. But first, I need to use the restroom. I'll be back in a minute," Kelly said, as she stood up and walked over to the door.

CHAPTER NINE

"Okay, let's get down to the business of who might have done this. The faster we can find that out, the faster we can get you out of this jail," Kelly said when she returned from the restroom.

"When my mother and dad came by earlier and told me you would be coming here, I thought you could post bail for me and get me out of here. Are you going to do that?" Zoe sked.

"No, Zoe," Finn said. "The judge is Ryan Murphy, and he's as hard-nosed as they come. Matter-of-fact, he's got red hair a lot like yours, and I've personally seen that he has a temper to match. He has a firm policy of no bail for anyone charged with murder. I'm sorry."

Didn't Liz mention the name Ryan when she was talking about Zoe's biological father? And he has red hair? Oh no, this would be the worst coincidence in the world. A judge overseeing his daughter's murder trial and doesn't know it's his daughter. I really don't know where to go with this, Kelly thought.

"So when can I get out of here?" Zoe asked.

"That depends. You're going to be arraigned Monday morning. As soon as we can find out who the murderer is and they're charged with Tina Lindsay's murder, you will be released. Until then I'm afraid this is going to be your new home away from home," Finn said.

Zoe remained quiet, and a tear trickled down her cheek. "Please, please do everything you can to find the murderer. I really am innocent. I don't want to stay here. I miss my family and my dog. Please help me."

"Zoe, speaking for Finn and myself, we will do everything we can to make sure you don't have to spend much time here, but I need to have a place to start. I need the names of anyone you think might have had a problem with Tina, whether it's a personal issue or a work-related issue. I've had a lot of experience solving cases like this, and I've never been unsuccessful. I don't intend for you to break my winning record," Kelly said with an encouraging sound in her voice.

"I'm going to start with the business," Zoe said, "and I'm pretty much shooting from the hip on this. Obviously, I know more about Tina and the business than her personal life.

"Tiffany Ruiz is the person in charge of the tasting room. My mother told me she was originally hired to work in the spa and did for about a week. Then Rosie, the person who had been in charge of the tasting room since it opened, had a personal emergency and had to leave on no notice. My mother told Tiffany that she'd have to work there a couple of days.

"But it turned out that Tiffany was a self-taught wine

scholar and with her in charge of the tasting room, sales shot through the roof. She was a natural salesperson whose knowledge sold the customers. That was about a year-and-a-half ago."

"I may be missing something here," Kelly said, "but I'm certainly not seeing any reason that she would be a suspect. Is there more?"

"Yes. You see, she always had this dream of working in a spa, actually, her dream was that she'd manage one someday. She personally told me that one evening when I went over to the tasting room to get a glass of wine after I'd finished for the day."

"Okay, so she wanted to work at a spa and she got sidetracked into being a wine person. Still, I think that's a pretty flimsy reason for her to want to murder Tina Lindsay," Finn said.

"I would agree with you except for one thing. She never lets up on wanting to work at the spa. Mom told me that Tiffany must ask her daily when she's going to be able to work at the spa, and she's done the same with me."

"Do you think Tiffany might have murdered Tina so she could take her place in the spa as the manager? Isn't that an awfully big leap for someone who's never worked there?" Kelly asked.

"Yes and no. Tiffany is extremely personable and very bright. People are drawn to her, and if it wasn't for her wine knowledge, she would have been moved back to the spa as soon as someone had been hired to replace Rosie. There is no doubt in my mind that she would make an excellent spa manager. If I were in charge of the whole operation, I'd put her in that position."

"If she's that successful in the wine part of the business, I would think your father would have a say about it," Finn said.

"And that's why she hasn't been moved over to the spa," Zoe said.

"What about her temperament. Do you think she's someone who could commit murder?" Kelly asked.

"I've never seen anything in her behavior that would lead me to think that she could commit murder. As a matter-of-fact I remember being in the tasting room one day and seeing her carry a spider outside and release it rather than kill it. She told me it was kind of a crazy thing, but she doesn't believe in killing bugs of any kind. It's a pretty far stretch to think of her killing a human being."

"Be that as it may," Finn said, "but I've certainly seen cases where the least-likeliest person was the one who did the evil deed. Kelly, put her on the list." He turned to Zoe and said, "Are you okay to continue with this? I'm sure this is exhausting after everything you've been through."

Kelly looked at him in surprise. She hadn't seen too many lawyers care that much about their client's emotional mood. She looked at Zoe and at Finn, then she looked at his right finger. No ring. She wondered if she was witnessing the beginning of something beyond a professional relationship when this ended.

Zoe smiled broadly at him and her green eyes lit up as

she said, "Thanks for caring. Yes, I am exhausted, but if this will help me get out of here any faster, than I want to continue."

She looked over at Kelly and said, "The only other person working at the spa who I think might be a candidate to be placed on the list is Raquelle DuBois. She's the assistant manager of the spa."

"And are you thinking that she might want be the manager of the spa? If so, that could be a possible motive," Finn said.

"With Raquelle, I don't know. She's very hard to read. She's very personable, and I know my mother thinks she's doing a good job. In fact, a while ago she had Raquelle take over all of the spa bookkeeping, so Tina would have more time to work on marketing, particularly internet marketing. I've not heard anything negative about her work."

"Zoe, you may not be saying anything negative about her, however I'm getting a feeling you don't care for her. Would I be right?" Kelly asked.

After taking a deep breath and visibly exhaling, Zoe said, "Yes, and I have no idea why. There's just something about her. I can't put my finger on it, but I don't trust her. And Finn, in answer to your question about Raquelle and whether or not she'd want to be the manager of the spa, I would think yes, although I've never heard her say that. If anything, she's somewhat subservient to Tina. You know, always asking if she can do anything for her or if she needs anything. I've always thought it was a bit much."

"Zoe, I'm not a whole lot older than you are," Finn said,

"but if I've learned one thing in practicing law, it's that we can never ignore our feelings. I really think that our emotions can glean things about people and situations long before our minds can."

He grinned and then said, "Maybe I should give up the practice of law and become a psychologist, because that kind of talk would get me kicked out of court. Anyway, Kelly, put Raquelle on your list. Any other people you can come up with who might have a motive?"

"No, I can't think of anyone who works here who would have a motive. Plus, Raquelle is not a warm fuzzy type of person. I don't think she interacts with many of the people who work at the resort."

"Alright, Zoe, do you know much about Tina's personal life?"

"No. I think you should talk to my parents about that. I know she's married, but other than that, I'm pretty clueless. Really, I think that's about it for now. If I think of someone else, I'll let you know."

Finn stood up and said, "Zoe, I'm sorry you had to go through this. Actually, I'm sorry you're having to go through all of this, but we will find out who did this and get you free. I promise you that. I'll come by tomorrow and see how you're doing." He turned to Kelly and said, "Ready?"

"Yes, and Zoe, I second what Finn just said. We will find out who the murderer is and get you out of here. I'm off to meet with your parents. Do you want me to deliver a message to them?"

Zoe thought for a moment, and then said, "Tell them I'm sorry they have to go through this, and that I'm innocent."

Finn looked at her and said, "Somehow I think they already know that. May I bring anything to you tomorrow? Hungry for anything?"

Okay, there is definitely an attraction here, even under these circumstances. Never have I heard an attorney ask his client if he could bring them some food. Now I have more of a reason than ever to find the person who did it. Hate to see young love denied, Kelly thought.

"No, I haven't been able to eat anything since they arrested me, and from what I've seen of the food here, that might be a good thing."

"Let me speak as a mother, Zoe," Kelly said. "It's important that you keep your strength up. We're going to need you to answer more questions as we get deeper into this investigation, so please try and eat."

Zoe looked at her and grinned, "Yes, Mom," she said.

CHAPTER TEN

When Finn and Kelly were outside the jail, he turned to her and said, "What did you think?"

"I don't think there's a shadow of a doubt that she's innocent. As to who did it, that's another story. I want to spend some time with Amy and Chris Jannette. I'm sure they can come up with the names of some other people who could possibly be suspects. Why don't I call you in the morning?"

"That would be fine. One thing I'm glad about is that Zoe is the only person in jail at the present time. I hope it stays that way. I'd hate for her to be subjected to some of the hard cases they get in there. She's far too good and innocent for that. Plus, as attractive as she is, she could be a real magnet for some sickos," Finn said.

"Yeah, I noticed that you seemed a bit taken with her beyond her just being your client," Kelly said with a grin. "Would I be right?"

"Was it that noticeable?" Finn asked with a worried look on his face. "Did I say or do something inappropriate?"

"No, Finn," Kelly said with a laugh, "but I think I better get to work so you can see about developing a relationship with Zoe that's outside of jail."

"Couldn't agree more. Here's my card with my cell number written on the back. If you find anything out from the Jannettes, give me a call. Otherwise, I'll talk to you tomorrow. Have a good evening."

"You, too," Kelly said as she walked over to Liz's car and opened the door.

"Well, how did it go? What's Zoe like?" Liz asked before she'd even started the car.

"Liz, Zoe is a wonderful young woman. You'd be very proud of her. Both Finn, that's the public defender's name, and who, by the way, I think might be interested in seeing more of your daughter once she's out of jail, and I firmly believe in her innocence. Now the problem is to find out who murdered Tina Lindsay."

"Was Zoe able to give you any names of people who she thinks might be considered as suspects?"

"Yes, she gave us the names of two people who work at Hillside. One is the assistant manager of the spa, and the other one works in the wine tasting rom. She knew nothing about Tina's personal life and suggested I talk to her parents, which I intend to do."

Liz started the car and backed out of her parking spot. "I pulled up the map to the Hillside Hotel on my phone. I think it will take us about twenty minutes to get there.

Kelly, while I'm driving, I'd really like for you to tell me everything about your meeting with Zoe. What does she look like? What did she sound like? Everything."

Which is exactly what Kelly did for the next twenty minutes with the exception of her suspicions about Judge Ryan Murphy. She knew it was something Liz would want to know, but for now she thought it was best to keep her suspicions to herself.

What was beginning to gnaw at Kelly was what would happen if she was unsuccessful in finding Tina's murderer? Was there something in the law that forbade a judge from presiding over a trial when a child of his was the defendant?

"Look, that must be it. See that big stone and wood building up ahead on the right?" Liz asked.

"Yes, and it's beautiful. You're right, there's a sign that says Hillside Resort. I guess that's kind of the catchall name for the three parts of it, the hotel, the spa, and the vineyard."

Liz entered a tree-lined road that led to the resort and into the hotel area. As she pulled up in front of the entrance, two valets opened their doors, and one of them said, "Will you ladies be staying as guests of the hotel tonight?"

"Yes, we will," Liz said.

"Fine, if you'll give me your name, I'll take your luggage to your room and park your car. Here's a claim ticket. When you need your car, just press the valet number on your room phone and your car will be waiting for you."

"My name is Kelly Reynolds," Liz said, deliberately choosing not to notice the expression on Kelly's face. "Where should I check in?"

"The reception desk is through that door on the left. See you in your room."

As they walked to the reception desk, Kelly whispered, "Why did you use my name and not yours?"

"Doc thought it would be better if my name was kept out of it for now. The reservation is in your name as well. I don't think anyone would know me from when I lived near here so many years ago, but it just seemed like a good idea to draw as little attention as possible to myself.

"Probably a good idea," Kelly said as they reached the reception counter which was far more than a desk, more like several yards of highly burnished mahogany.

"How may I help you ladies?" a woman behind the counter asked.

"My name is Kelly Reynolds, and I believe that the Jannettes made a reservation for me."

"Let me check on that, Mrs. Reynolds. Give me just a moment." She typed on her computer for a moment and then said, "Lovely, you'll be staying in the Presidential Suite. Here's the elevator cardkey, and here's the room cardkey. It's the first elevator over there. The elevator will take you directly to your suite.

"Mrs. Jannette asked that you please call her when you get settled, and that she's very anxious to talk to you. You can use the house phone to call her at this number. I hope you enjoy your stay with us. The spa has about any treatment you would want, and the tasting room for the vineyard is open until 8:00 tonight. If we can do anything to make your stay more enjoyable, please call the desk."

As they walked over to the elevators, Kelly said, "I can see why this resort has a five-star rating. So far, the service has been impeccable."

"Yeah, just stay out of the jacuzzi," Liz said with a grin, the first grin Kelly had seen on her face today.

The elevator only went to the Presidential Suite, and opened into a small foyer with a large round table located in the center. A vase of fresh orchids was displayed in the center of the table. Two large mahogany doors were beyond it and a prominent brass plaque on one of the doors was engraved with the words "Presidential Suite."

Kelly put her cardkey in the slot, and as the door opened into a large living room, they both gasped. The view in front of them was phenomenal, a floor-to-ceiling panoramic view of the area's vineyards and far in the distance, a ridge of mountains.

The suite had a full kitchen, dining area, and two suites, one on each side of the living room. The bathrooms in each suite had a full bath, a Japanese wooden soaking tub, and a tiled shower with sixteen jets which one could choose to use individually or en masse.

There were numerous bottles of lotions, bath salts, and other items from the spa. The towels were so thick it looked like someone had forgotten to unfold them when they'd placed them on the warming rods. Luxurious white shag throw rugs were located throughout the suite, contrasting beautifully with the golden oak floors.

"Kelly, I may not ever leave here, but make me a promise," Liz said, as she ran her hands over the towels.

"I'll try. What is it?"

"Promise me when this is over and we find the murderer, or you do, that you and I come here for a vacation," she said.

"I'll do you one better. When we find out who the murderer is, we'll probably be hosted for free, and we can bring Doc and Mike. How does that sound?" Kelly asked.

"Even better. Now I think you better call Amy and Chris. They're probably nervous wrecks by now."

CHAPTER ELEVEN

"Mrs. Jannette? This is Kelly Reynolds," she said as she spoke into the hotel's house phone.

"Kelly, I'm so glad you're here, and please, call me Amy and my husband, Chris. I trust your accommodations are satisfactory."

"Beyond, Amy, totally beyond. Thank you very much. First of all, I want to tell you what a lovely daughter you have. And let me reassure you and your husband that her public defender, Finn O'Conner, and I will find the murderer, so your daughter can be set free. We are both absolutely convinced of her innocence."

"Thank you for that, Kelly. It means a lot. We are so indebted to you for coming here on practically no notice and agreeing to help us. I understand that we are also indebted to your son for being able to exert some pressure on someone to be able to get Mr. O'Conner to defend Zoe."

"I'll tell him that, and I have no idea who Cash talked to or what he did, but I guess that's one of the perks of being a Senator. Actually, this is the first time I've seen it in action, since he hasn't been a Senator all that long."

"Kelly, obviously Chris and I are anxious to talk to you, but we don't want to push you. I know it's already dinnertime, so if you'd prefer to talk to us after you eat dinner, that would be fine. If not, we'd love for you to join us here at our house for a glass of wine so we can talk. We live on the grounds, and it's only a short walk."

"I'm all for talking now, Amy, and I'm sure Liz would agree with me. I'd also love a glass of pinot noir. My husband is always telling me that the best pinot noirs come from this region of the state. How do we find your house?"

"If you look out your window, you'll see a number of buildings on the right side and the left side of a large stone center walkway. Our house is the one at the far left end. It will be getting dark soon, but the path is well lit, and this is a very safe area." Then she laughed and said, "Well, it was until the other night, but we still feel it's very safe."

"I'm sure it is," Kelly said. "We'll be there shortly. Right now, we need to take a moment to enjoy this gorgeous sunset we can see from our window. From this view it's spectacular. I have a friend who would call this a 'God wink.' See you in a few minutes."

Liz looked over at her, a puzzled expression on her face, and then said, "A God wink? That I've never heard of. What is it?"

"It's that moment just before the sun sinks on the horizon and kind of kisses everything or winks at it. And that's what's happening right now."

"That's charming, Kelly. Where did you ever come up with that phrase?"

"A friend of mine always used that phrase in describing a sunset, and it stuck with me as being entirely appropriate."

A few minutes later they rode the elevator down to the ground floor and then followed Amy's directions to their house. The door was open and Amy said, "Welcome, come in. And, yes, that sunset was spectacular."

"Agreed. I'm Kelly, and this is Liz. It's wonderful to meet both of you. We have a question. On the walk here we saw the spa, but we didn't see a sign for the jacuzzi. Is it on the side of the building or attached to the rear?"

"It's on the side, not far from the parking lot for the spa. It has a separate entrance, because some people just prefer to use it and not go through the main spa. The sauna is set up in the same way," Chris said. "But before we talk any more, let me get you a glass of our pinot noir. It's won several awards, and I think it's the best one we've ever produced."

He walked over to a sideboard with a number of bottles of wine on it and poured each of them a glass. Kelly swirled it, took a sip, and said, "Chris, Amy, even if you weren't here, I would say that this is the best wine I've ever had. I must buy a couple of bottles of this for my husband. He would love it."

"I second that," Liz said. "And I want to tell you what a pleasure it is to finally meet you. I can tell from the things that you've sent me over the years that you've done a wonderful job raising Zoe. As hard as it was for me to let her go, obviously it was the best decision I could have made for her." She held her wine glass up to them in a mock toast.

"Thank you, Liz. That means so much to Chris and me, but Zoe has been a wonderful child. She has such a bright future, and I just want this behind her so she can get on with her life. We thank you from the bottom of our hearts for making the decision you did regarding her. She's definitely the best thing that ever happened to us."

"Did both you and Kelly meet with her?" Amy asked.

"No, I didn't think it would be appropriate for either Zoe or me," Liz said. "If we do meet, and we'll cross that bridge when we come to it, I'd rather it wasn't when she was in jail. I'm sure she would have been mortified to meet her biological mother in that manner."

"That was a very gracious thing of you to do, Liz, thank you," Amy said. "I think she's under enough stress as it is."

Just then there was a knock on the door and Chris stepped away to answer it. A moment later they heard him say, "Thanks," and a beautiful Belgian Malinois followed Chris into the room. He looked at Liz and at Kelly, then came over to both of them, sniffing them carefully. They were both dog people and knew enough to put their hands out so he could get a sense of them.

He must have decided that they'd passed some test known only to dogs, because he laid down at Kelly's feet and promptly went to sleep.

"I can tell that he likes both of you," Chris said. "Normally, it takes a lot longer for him to decide how he feels about someone, and I've never seen him secure enough to go to sleep next to someone who's a visitor in the house."

"What's this handsome boy's name?" Kelly asked.

"This is Nico. He's Zoe's dog, and I had one of our employees take him for a long walk because Zoe takes him for one every day. She inherited him from a friend. He was a K-9 dog, and as such, is highly trained. Amy and I were fine with her getting a dog, because her home is a little farther away from ours and somewhat isolated."

"Yes, she told me about him today," Kelly said.

"Speaking of today, Amy and I would like you to tell us everything you can about your meeting with Zoe and the public defender."

"Certainly. Here's what happened." Kelly spent the next twenty minutes relating what took place during her meeting with Zoe and Finn. She told them about her feeling that they may be seeing more of Finn when this was all over.

They both laughed, and then Kelly said, "I mentioned the names that Zoe came up with as possible suspects, but since she told me she really didn't know anything about Tina's personal life, I'd like to hear from both of you about it. I'd also like to know if there's anyone in the area who might want to see the resort get bad publicity."

"First of all," Chris said. "I can save you the trouble of investigating Tiffany." He looked at Amy and said, "And I haven't even had a chance to tell you about this."

"About what?" Amy asked.

"The afternoon of Tina's murder, I was in the tasting room with Tiffany. I told her what a great job she was doing, and said that I knew she wanted to work at the spa, but I had a proposition for her. I told her I didn't want to lose her, and was afraid she might go to the Merritt Spa and ask for a job there."

"That's something I hadn't even thought of," Amy said.

"I told her I would not only give her a raise, but I would give her a percent of the sales she was responsible for, kind of a sales commission on the things she sold, if you will. She was thrilled and told me she'd been so frustrated for so long because she'd always wanted to work at the spa, but in the last couple of weeks something had shifted, and she realized she had a talent for working with wine and liked it. She said she'd been looking for the right time to ask me if there was any way she could become more involved in the creation of the wine.

"We agreed that I would appoint her to be my wine assistant and every week she would spend a day with me, learning the business of making wine. She was thrilled and laughingly told me she'd even harbored evil thoughts of how she could get rid of Tina, so she could be the spa manager, but for whatever reason, there had been a change, and now she was really looking forward to this new challenge."

"Chris, that's wonderful," Amy said. "She really does have a natural gift for wine. I'm so glad it worked out. Zoe loves to taste the wines, but she doesn't have, at least that I know of, any desire to become more involved in that part of the resort. Plus, she'll be busy enough with the spa and the hotel. That's great news."

"I certainly thought so. As for Tina's personal life. You might want to take a look at her husband. His name is Brett Lindsay. They were married right after high school. He had some bad luck in his last football game in high school. A guy tackled him, and his left leg was shattered. There went his hopes for the future. He had a college football scholarship all lined up, but that went south because of his leg injury.

"He'd worked at his father's little hardware store most of his life on the weekends, and it was about that time that his father became ill and asked him to take over the store for him. I suppose some would say it was a blessing, because it was about the only job he could get. It's not like there are a lot of jobs available in this area. Our resort hires more people than any other business in the valley."

"Did you hire Tina or was she already working here when you bought the resort?"

"She was working here when the previous owners had it, so the answer is yes, she was employed here at the resort when we acquired it. Eventually she worked her way up to become the spa manager, which was far better than Brett did. His father passed away, and Brett really had no choice but to continue working at the hardware store. I don't think it does more than make ends meet, but at least it gives Brett a reason to get up in the morning and gives him something to do."

"Would you say they had a good marriage?" Kelly asked.

"Who knows?" Chris said. He was quiet for several moments as if he was deciding whether or not he should say something. Then he said, "I did overhear a conversation at the coffee shop recently that makes me think not."

"You never told me that," Amy said. "What did you hear?"

"Well, I don't like to spread gossip, but there may be something relevant to what I heard. It was just last week, and I was having a little lunch at the coffee shop. I overheard the cook and the waitress, that would be Maisie and Joe, say something about Brett. I was seated at the back near the kitchen and was easily able to hear their conversation.

"The coffee shop is next door to Lindsay Hardware, Brett's hardware store. Maisie, the waitress, said she was getting tired of seeing the open sign on the door of the hardware store turned to closed whenever some woman went in. Joe agreed with her, but then said for the last few months it's always been the same woman, you know, that assistant manager at the spa."

"Do you think he meant our spa?" Amy asked.

"I don't know. I've been thinking about it ever since. Of course, our assistant is Raquelle. If it's her, and if she's the one who's been seeing Brett, she might have a motive for murder."

"I'm glad you told me," Kelly said. "I definitely need to

look into her. But I'm curious, Amy. You said the words 'our spa'. Does that mean there is another spa located in the area?"

"Yes. It's a few miles from here, the Merritt Spa. The poor guy who owns it has been trying for years to get some development company to build a hotel attached to it, so he could make it a destination resort, instead of a day spa. He's even approached us about having his spa become a satellite of ours."

"And what did you say?"

"Quite frankly, we didn't see any reason to. We have a large clientele and with the constant changeover in guests at the hotel who are looking for a full resort experience, our spa is always full. There didn't seem to be any benefit to us. His spa is attractive, and I know that some of our guests go there, particularly the ones I call spa groupies. They're the ones who go from spa to spa. It's kind of a hobby of theirs."

"What about the owner? Could he possibly be a suspect?" Kelly asked.

"I wouldn't think so, but then again I never thought Zoe would be a suspect in a murder case. His name is Cody Merritt. Nice enough guy. He does a good job. As a matter of fact, several of the people who work for us also work for him."

"What about if he wanted to discredit Hillside Spa in hopes that he would get some of your spa business? Maybe he thought a scandal involving your spa would do it?" Kelly asked.

"I suppose that's a possibility, but how long would that work for?" Amy asked. "I'm sure some of our guests will avoid the jacuzzi for a while and maybe even the spa, but I don't think it will have much of a long-term adverse effect on the spa.

"And something else I've been thinking about while we've been talking. If someone wanted to do something to hurt your spa's reputation, why single out Tina and murder her? What difference would it make who the person killed at the spa was, if that was their intention? And they could have done it anywhere on the grounds. I would think that doing it in the jacuzzi was certainly riskier for them than other places would have been. To me, it seems personal to Tina."

"That's a very good point, Amy. Chris, can you think of anyone else who could possibly be a suspect?"

Both Amy and Chris were quiet for several moments, thinking. Then they both shook their heads. Chris finally said, "I really can't think of anyone else, and I can see that Amy can't either. If we do, we'll give you a call."

"I'd appreciate it. Here's my card. My cell phone is on it. One last question, and then I think we need to get something to eat in the hotel restaurant. It's been a long day. What do you know about the sheriff who arrested Zoe, Dirk Kuyper?"

"I think he's a good guy," Chris said. "I've heard that he wants to move up and is very ambitious. Other than that, I've never heard anything that would be considered a black mark against him. Any special reason you're asking?"

"It just strikes me as odd that he would have made an arrest on so little evidence. I mean a couple of people hearing an argument and two people seeing Zoe leave the jacuzzi, if they actually did see that, and remember, it was at night and visibility was limited. I just have my doubts."

"Why is that?" Chris asked.

"Because she was near the jacuzzi when she was walking Niko. I'm thinking that's what they saw, and in their mind, it translated to seeing her walk out the door. Anyway, I'm wondering if he made the arrest hoping to gain some notoriety for quickly solving a murder mystery."

"But if Zoe went to trial and was acquitted, wouldn't that make him look bad?" Amy asked.

"Unquestionably, and that's why I think he's trying to ramrod this case through. If we can't solve it quickly, and it comes to that, I would imagine that the sheriff or someone else will put pressure on Amy to plea bargain, admitting to the murder in exchange for a lesser sentence."

"It just can't go that far, Kelly," Chris said. "I know she didn't do it, and that's just wrong. Kelly, please do everything you can to solve this quickly. I don't want her to have to go through a trial."

"Nor do I. One thing I did find out from my son. He told me Finn O'Conner is one of the best attorneys practicing in this area. He said he was as good as any you could hire privately, so at least that's good news, but I refuse to let it go that far."

Kelly turned to Liz and said, "It's time for us to get

some dinner, because I need to do some work on my laptop later, and I also want to call Mike." She turned back to Amy and Chris and said, "That's my husband. He's the sheriff of Beaver County, and I intend to ask him to do some searches on the people we've put on our suspect list as well as Sheriff Kuyper. As a law enforcement person, he's able to access information I can't."

"Kelly," Chris said as he stood up. "Amy and I will never be able to thank you enough for what you're doing. We talked about it earlier, and we'd like you to take this check. If we hired a private investigator, we'd have paid them. It's only fair that you're compensated for this."

"I appreciate the offer, but the answer is no thanks. I'm doing this because Liz and Doc are my closest friends, not for any monetary gain. If you want to do something at the end of this, you can comp us a couple of rooms at the hotel for a night. We were talking earlier and think our husbands would love it here."

"Consider it done," Amy said. "And by the way, I highly recommend the baked boneless pork chops. They're my favorite thing on the menu."

"Thanks, that sounds like just what this hungry person needs. Goodnight Niko," Kelly said as she reached down and petted the big dog, then she and Liz left.

CHAPTER TWELVE

"I don't need anything in our room," Kelly said as she and Liz walked back to the hotel. "Okay with you if we just go straight to the restaurant?"

"Absolutely. I was able to eat a little bit of lunch at your coffeeshop today, but for the first time since I got the call, I'm hungry."

A few moments later they entered the Chef's Table at the Hillside, a gourmet restaurant located in the hotel. Kelly walked over to the hostess and said, "We don't have a reservation. Is there any chance we could get a table?"

"Are you Kelly Reynolds?" the hostess asked.

"I am," she answered, wondering how the hostess would know her name.

"Mrs. Jannette just called and told me to make sure you and your friend were seated. Please follow me," the hostess said.

She led them to a window table which had the same

view as the one from their suite, only now it was dark. Their waiter brought them menus, and they both ordered a glass of the Hillside pinot noir.

"Well, Kelly, are you going to follow Amy's recommendation and order the boneless pork chop?" Liz asked as she took a sip of her wine.

"I am. I figure if the owner of a five-star restaurant says that something is good, it probably is. I'm also going to have a shrimp cocktail and the asparagus with a light sweet sauce. And I'm going to splurge for dessert and have the chocolate cake!" Kelly said as she closed her menu and set it on the table.

The waitress approached their table and said, "Are you ready to order?"

"Yes," Kelly said, and gave the waitress her choices.

The waitress looked over at Liz and said, "And you, ma'am?"

"I'll have exactly what she's having," Liz said as she sat back. The waitress left and Liz said, "So, now that you've been able to get some information on the case, what do you think?"

Kelly took a sip of her wine and then said, "I want to check with Mike. I'm curious what he knows about the sheriff, and I'd like him to run a check on the names we have. I also want to do a detailed social media search and see if I can find out anything."

"Any shoot from the hip guesses?"

"I hate to make a judgement about people until I've had a chance to talk to them, but I do feel the sheriff arrested Zoe without any real strong evidence that she was the one who did it. He's charging her for murder based on what people have said. You know in law enforcement there's the concept of the 'smoking gun'."

"I've heard the term, but I don't think I've ever heard it really explained. What, exactly, is it?" Liz asked as the waitress brought them their shrimp cocktails.

"It means that there has to be indisputable proof or evidence in a crime. I'm not seeing that here. The smoking gun is exactly that. For example, if it was proven that Zoe had possession of the gun that murdered Tina, if in fact that's what happened that would definitely fit the definition. But so far, unless the sheriff has evidence that hasn't been disclosed, I think this is about the flimsiest case and reason for an arrest that I've ever seen," Kelly said as she brought a piece of shrimp up to her mouth.

They were both quiet for a few moments as they enjoyed the shrimp cocktail and then began on the asparagus and pork which was served with Lyonnaise potatoes. Kelly thought it was the perfect accompaniment to the main course.

"Kelly, I can see your mind working. You're trying to decide whether you could serve this at the coffee shop, right?"

"You know me too well, Liz," Kelly said. "Yes, I'm pretty sure I can work this out, but I'll probably have to try it out on Mike a few times before I offer it at the coffee shop."

"Shall I tell Doc to look for it?" Liz asked with a grin.

"Yes, I definitely think it's doable."

The waitress cleared the table and then brought them their chocolate dessert. They were both quiet as they ate it. Then Liz said, "While you're at it, try and recreate this. It's fabulous."

"Agreed." She nodded toward the waitress and made a motion with her hand as if she was writing, an international sign for "Please bring the check."

The waitress walked over to the table and said, "Your dinner has been taken care of by Mrs. Jannette. Is there anything else I can bring either of you?"

"No, thank you. Wonderful food and excellent service."

"My pleasure," she said as she walked away.

"Kelly, we need to leave her a generous tip," Liz said, opening her purse and taking out some cash. "This is my treat and the least I can do for upending your schedule."

"Thanks. I'm ready to head up to our suite," Kelly said.

CHAPTER THIRTEEN

Kelly stuck her keycard in the slot on the door to their suite. When they walked in, Liz said, "Looks like the maid has been here. The lamps are on, and there's a fire in the fireplace. Lovely. Wonder if there will be a chocolate on my pillow? Think I'll go in and look, then I need to put on something more comfortable. I'm still wearing my psychologist suit from when I got dressed this morning to go to work."

"Let's go find out about the chocolate. Liz, after you get changed, why don't you come back in here. I need to talk to you about something."

"For some reason I don't like the sound of that, Kelly. Want to give me a hint?"

"No. I'll meet you back here in a few minutes."

Kelly brought the chocolate that was on her pillow into the kitchen and poured herself a glass of water, then she went into the living room to wait for Liz. She'd been debating how she should tell Liz about Judge Murphy, who she suspected was Zoe's father, and had come to the conclusion that she'd just tell her what she knew.

She hoped her fears were groundless, and he wasn't Zoe's father, but everything she knew so far about him led her to believe he was. The thing that clinched it had been when Finn had mentioned the red hair.

"Okay, I'm here. I fortified myself with a glass of port I saw on the bar. I had a feeling I'd need it."

"Liz, what I'm going to tell you is sheer speculation on my part. But I do have reason to think it might possibly be true."

"Kelly, that's about the strangest introduction to a subject I've ever heard. Please, get to the meat of it."

"You asked for it. I was prepared to do it a little more gently. I have reason to believe the judge in Zoe's case is her biological father."

Liz's eyes became as wide as saucers, and then she said, "You must be kidding. What makes you say that?"

"First of all, on the way here you happened to mention that her father's name was Ryan, right?"

"Yes, I did," Liz said.

"Today, when Finn and I were talking before we met with Zoe, he mentioned that the judge's name was Ryan Murphy."

When Kelly said the name, Liz visibly paled and clutched her throat. "No, that can't be. There must be another lawyer with that name. Murphy was the last name of the man who is her father. Maybe it's just some strange twist of fate, a coincidence if you will."

"When he said the name, I hoped so, although I didn't know that was her father's last name. Remember earlier, Liz, when we were in the car after we left the jail and you told me you wanted to know everything about Zoe, such as what she looked like? And I told you about her flaming red hair. Did her biological father have red hair?"

Liz was quiet for several moments and then said in a very quiet voice, "Yes. It was probably his most distinguishing feature. But why do you ask? Because Zoe has red hair? That could just be fluke."

"Liz, Finn made some comment about what a tough judge Ryan Murphy is, and went on to say his temper matched his red hair. I started putting two and two together, and given that the judge is from this area, I came up with the thought that he probably is Zoe's father."

Tears began to gather in Liz's eyes, and she grabbed a tissue from a box on the table next to her and wiped at them. "Kelly, I'm really speechless. And I do agree with you. The chances of there being two men named Ryan Murphy with red hair who are lawyers in this area are pretty impossible. So, now what?"

"I've been thinking about this ever since it occurred to me. The thing that really upsets me is thinking that Judge Murphy could preside over a trial in which his daughter would be the defendant. I have no idea what the laws are regarding something like this."

"Kelly, we can't tell anyone about him being her father.

What can we possibly do to prevent it?"

"I'm not a lawyer, but I would think if a judge found out his daughter was a defendant in a case he was overseeing, he would have to, I think the word is, recuse himself. In other words, step away from the case."

"Yes, but wouldn't everyone know then and the reason he stepped away would become public?"

"I don't know the answer to that, but my gut instinct is yes. And who would tell him since his child doesn't even know that he's her father? Finn, me, you? I honestly have no idea," Kelly said.

"This is just as bad as finding out that Zoe was charged with murder. Maybe worse," Liz said. "This whole thing could blow up, and Zoe's whole personal history would become public knowledge. There has to be a way out of this, Kelly. What can we do? By the way, did you tell Finn about your suspicions?"

"No, it wasn't my story to tell. It's yours. I think there is a way out of it, but we're going to have to do everything we can in the next couple of days to find the murderer.

"Here's my thinking. If we can find the murderer by Sunday night and convince Sheriff Kuyper to arrest whoever it is, he'll have to release Zoe. There will be no arraignment for her, and she'll never have to appear in front of Judge Murphy."

"That would be a good thing. I mean what if she looked at him and saw some feature or trait that she had. She might begin to put two and two together," Liz said. "If so, maybe she'd confront him, and he'd find out that way that he was her father, although she doesn't know her biological father's name. I'm the only one who does. I didn't put it on the birth certificate."

"Still, it could get messy at that point," Kelly said. "No, we need to find the murderer ASAP. I'm going in my bedroom and do what I said earlier, call Mike and then do some social media research. You can help me to save time. Research Judge Ryan Murphy as to age, where he went to law school, maybe check out his Facebook page. Let's start by finding out if, in fact, he is Zoe's father."

"Not a problem. I'll get on it right now. Anything else?"

"Yes, I want you to research Cody Merritt. He's the man who owns the Merritt Spa. I think you should call him early tomorrow and tell him you're a reporter doing a story on spas in the wine country and would like to interview him.

"Egos being what they are, more than likely he'll be anxious for the publicity. If there's any way you could find out where he was on the night of the murder, that would be hugely advantageous. After I finish working tonight, I'll probably have some other things for you to do. With both of us researching, it will go a lot faster and hopefully, we can solve this case before the arraignment."

"Okay, I'll be back in a little while, and you can give me some more marching orders," Liz said, with a smile on her face.

CHAPTER FOURTEEN

"Hi, love, it's me," Kelly said when Mike answered his cell phone. "I need to run some things by you, and I could use your help."

"I'm all ears. How is it going?" he asked.

"Difficult, although I did have a pinot noir wine that you would love. I'll buy some bottles and bring them to you. Let me give you a recap of what I've found out. It's a little different from most cases, because there is an upsetting emotional aspect to it as well. One that Liz knew nothing about when she asked for my help. I was the one who had to tell her, and it was very difficult.

"Let's get started then," Mike said. "The sooner you can wind up this thing, the sooner you can come home. Rebel, Lady, and Skyy are nervously pacing around, wondering where you are," he said referring to their three dogs.

"Alright. I'll go with the case first. Here's what I've found out so far." Kelly spent the next twenty minutes going over her meetings with Finn, Zoe, and the Jannettes.

"Mike, if you could spend some time running those people through the various law enforcement sites I can't get into, I'd really appreciate it. I know the computer in your office there at the house is set up to do that. Any chance you could do it tonight and call me in the morning?"

"Sure. I worked late and just took a frozen casserole out of the freezer. That's the extent of my plans for tonight. I'll get on it as soon as we end this call. What else do you have?"

"Have you ever heard of a sheriff by the name of Dirk Kuyper?"

"Yes, why?"

"He's the one who arrested Zoe, and I think based on what I just told you about the facts of the case, that he really doesn't have anything solid. It sounds like an arrest that isn't backed up by a lot of facts that will stick."

"I would agree with you. And yes, I have heard of him. Actually, I met him at a conference in Portland last year, and I thought he was insufferable. He was so full of himself it was hard to be around him, and believe me, he could have cared less about me.

"The man had one thing on his mind and that was where his next gig was going to be. He is definitely angling for something higher up than being a county sheriff in some rural county.

"He spent the whole conference sidling up to anyone he thought might be important to him, and obviously I wasn't.

The only reason I did get to meet him was that seats had been assigned for the day of talks by various law enforcement people, and he was seated next to me. I think the sole extent of my conversation with him concerned me passing him the carafe of water that was in front of me.

"Do I think he'd arrest someone hoping to get notoriety? Oh yeah, but the good news is that a good local county district attorney would want the case dropped after the arraignment, and he'd had a chance to look at the case. He'd see that he didn't have a chance of making a conviction, and would ask the judge to dismiss the charges, and then it would all be over," Mike said.

"Not necessarily," Kelly said. "Here's the second part of what I found out today, the emotional part." She told him what she suspected about Judge Murphy and his relationship to Zoe.

Mike was quiet for several moments, and then said, "How is Liz handling this? And what if there are two men named Ryan Murphy who are attorneys and have red hair. I mean, it could happen."

"I know, and I asked Liz to get on the internet and find out everything she could about him. Mike, I've never felt so sure of anything in my life, and there is no way that Zoe should ever appear before Judge Murphy if that's so."

"If he is her biological father, I would agree, but that's still a big if. There's a chance that this is all just a big coincidence."

"Mike, the chances of that are slim to none, and in my mind 'Slim just left town'. I'm going to operate under the firm belief that Judge Murphy is her father, and if I can't find out who murdered Tina Lindsay by Sunday night, I'm going to be looking at having some of the worst discussions with people I've ever had in my life. People like Zoe, Zoe's parents, the public defender, and the judge. Can you imagine just how fun that's going to be?"

"In that case, let's get off the phone so we both can get to work. What are you planning next?" Mike asked.

"I'm going to spend some time doing social media research and see if I can come up with anything. I know it's a long shot, but at least it will give me something to do. Liz is researching Judge Murphy. We're looking at where he went to law school, his age, things like that, although we're both pretty sure what she'll find.

"I also asked Liz to make an appointment with the spa owner I mentioned under the excuse she's a reporter and doing a story on spas in the area. It's not much, but I couldn't think of another way to get to him.

"Figured if one of us made an appointment for a treatment at his spa, the only thing we'd really see would be the person who was giving us the treatment, and that would be it. He's a longshot, but this has become so personal, I can't rule anyone out."

"How's Liz taking this, Kelly?"

"I think she's devastated. First to have her daughter charged with murder, and then the whole father thing. It's really pretty unbelievable, but I'm seeing it up close and personal. This is one of the few times I wish I'd never solved a case. I have no idea how this is going to end, and

I'm really afraid people are going to be terribly hurt."

"Yeah, I can see how you'd feel that way. Would you like me to come up there? I don't know what I could do to help, but maybe something."

"Thanks, Mike, but no. Liz and I will get through this, however it turns out, but it occurs to me that Liz has probably told Doc what's happening. I'm sure he's pretty worried about her. Might be nice to ask him over for dinner or go out to dinner with him."

"I'll call him right now. And before we sign off, heard from your son when he got home from the capitol this evening. He wondered how you were doing, and I told him I hadn't heard from you yet, but expected to momentarily. I'll call him and let him know you're okay."

"That's fine, Mike, but I do have a favor to ask."

"Sure, what is it?"

"Tell him I'm really happy with Finn, but don't mention anything about the judge and my suspicions. I really think this is a case where the fewer people who know about it, the better everyone affected by it will be."

"I agree. Try and get some sleep, and I'll call you about 8:00 tomorrow morning and fill you in on what I've found out. Loves."

"And loves to you. Give the dogs a hug and a kiss for me."

"I'd feel more comfortable with a pat. Okay by you?"

"Sure, macho man. Good night."

Kelly spent the next two hours researching Cody Merritt, Tiffany Ruiz, Brett Lindsay, and Raquelle DuBois. She'd just finished, feeling it had been a waste of time, when she heard a knock on her door.

"Come in," Kelly called out.

Liz walked in and said, "Did I catch you at a good place or would you rather talk to me later?"

"No, now is fine. I just spent two hours and don't have much to show for it, other than I thought of something else I'd like you to do tomorrow. So, what did you find out about the judge?" Kelly asked.

Liz sat down, sighed deeply, and looked at Kelly with sad eyes. "There's no doubt that Judge Murphy is the man who impregnated me and is Zoe's father. Everything matches. His age. His college and law school education. Where he grew up. Everything. There was even a picture of him on his Facebook page, so there is absolutely no doubt in my mind."

Kelly sat back and looked at her friend, searching for the right words to say to her. "Liz, I can't possibly know how you feel right now. This is like a scene out of a soap opera, but if nothing else, it just intensifies my desire to find the murderer. I don't want you or Zoe to have to go through her finding out that Judge Murphy is her father. I promise I will do everything in my power to ensure that it doesn't happen. We will find out who murdered Tina."

"Kelly, there's something else I found out. Ryan is

married, although I found nothing indicating that he had children. But if this does become public, can you imagine how this would upend his world? I rather doubt that he ever told his wife about me or the fact that I was going to have a baby. I mean, what would be the point? This is just a terrible, terrible situation, and rest assured, I'm going to do whatever I can to help you."

"Okay. As tragic a situation as this is, we need to keep going. Sitting here talking isn't going to help us solve the case. Right now, or rather as soon as we get up tomorrow, we need to get in action."

"I'm planning on calling Mr. Merritt about 9:00. I'm afraid if I call any earlier, he won't be at the spa yet," Liz said. "You mentioned earlier that you had something else for me to do. What is it?"

"Remember how Chris mentioned he'd overheard the cook and the waitress in that coffee shop talking about how whenever a certain woman went into Brett Lindsay's hardware store, he turned the sign on the door from open to closed? I'd like you to go to the coffee shop after you get through interviewing Mr. Merritt and see what you can find out about Brett."

"Any tips on how to do that?"

"Well, in a town this small, I imagine that the coffee shop has no more than one or two waitresses. Let's hope you get lucky and get the same one that Chris overheard. Maybe you could say something about you'd needed to go to the hardware store, but every time you stopped by, the sign had been turned to closed. Maybe ask what the usual hours were. Something like that. You're the psychologist.

You'll figure something out."

"Sounds good. I can do that. What are your plans for tomorrow?" Liz asked.

"First of all, I need to talk to Mike. He's doing some research for me. As a law professional, he has sources he can use that I can't access. Based on what he tells me, I'll kind of go from there. I'd thought earlier that I should talk to Tiffany Ruiz, but based on what Chris told us, I don't think that will be necessary. I've pretty much crossed her off of our suspect list. I need to talk to Raquelle DuBois, but I don't know if she works on Saturdays. Now, we both need to go to bed. The next couple of days are going to be busy."

"I know," Liz said, "and I'm exhausted, but I do have a question."

"Sure, what?"

"Has the thought crossed your mind that all of this could be in vain, that the murderer was just some random guest at the hotel who gets his or her jollies from killing people?"

"I hadn't thought of it in quite that way, but yes, the thought has occurred to me that it could be a random thing. But quite frankly the odds of that being the case are low, because most murders are committed by people who know the victim. Let's operate under that assumption. Now, good night."

"Good night, Kelly."

CHAPTER FIFTEEN

Kelly's mind had been whirling all night, and when she woke up at 6:30 the next morning, she was still tired. She stumbled to the kitchen and made a pot of coffee, hoping the caffeine would revive her. She carried a cup back to her room and quickly showered, figuring that Mike would be calling shortly.

She'd finished showering and was just carrying her second cup of coffee into her room, when her cell phone rang. "Morning, Mike, I thought you were the only one who would be calling me this early."

"I would hope so. I'd hate to hear that your other boyfriends were calling this early," he said with a laugh.

"Fat chance, those days have come and gone," she said. "How are you and the dogs doing?"

"All's well at the Reynolds casa. Dogs have been fed and put out. I'm drinking a cup of coffee, and ready to fill you in on what I found out."

"Good. Hope you have something I can use. After I

talked to you, I spent a couple of hours doing research on the people on my list of suspects, but didn't find out anything of interest.

"Liz came in when I was finished and she had determined, through her research on the judge in the case, that he is the man who impregnated her and is the father of Zoe. Everything was a match, where he grew up, where he went to school, age, etc. The term beyond a reasonable doubt comes to mind and it is beyond a reasonable doubt."

"That certainly is a distraction you don't need," Mike said. "Let me tell you what I came up with. There is no doubt that my assessment of Sheriff Kuyper was correct. I found a number of newspaper articles where his name was mentioned as someone wanting to move up in law enforcement circles. There was even one that mentioned he had a law degree and would be an excellent choice for Oregon Attorney General.

"I doubt if that will happen, since he has no courtroom experience beyond what I do, testifying in court at trials when we've been involved in an arrest of the defendant. However, he is very, very ambitious, and I sure wouldn't put it past him to try to solve a case as quick as possible with the hope that the defendant would plea bargain, rather than go to trial. That would be a win for him, regardless of the lives it would affect," Mike said.

"When I heard what the evidence was that was used as a reason to arrest Zoe and put her in jail, I thought it was just not enough. But be that as it may, because of the problem with Zoe and the judge, this case cannot go to trial or even to an arraignment," Kelly said.

"I fully agree. I pulled up Tiffany Ruiz and found nothing. She's never been arrested, no history of any problems with the law, absolutely nothing. Of course that doesn't rule her out, but there's nothing that would indicate she might be the person you're looking for."

"I've taken her off of my suspect list. She did want to work at the spa and maybe she thought the only way she could get there was by getting rid of Tina, but from what Chris told me, that's no longer the case."

"Based on what I saw when I did a computer background check on her, I'd have to agree," Mike said. "I did some work on Cody Merritt, too. I found out that he's been trying to get a developer to build a hotel on his land for a number of years. He's had a few traffic tickets, and he's been divorced twice, but other than that, I didn't find anything that would indicate he's your murderer."

"Maybe he just snapped out of frustration," Kelly said. "I imagine trying that long and hard to get something going would wear a person down. It's hard to believe, but…"

"Could be. As you well know, anything could be, but it's not likely. Remember the old saying about going for the low-hanging fruit? Those two may be in that category, but I wouldn't waste my time on either one of them. So saying, the next two are interesting."

"How so?" Kelly asked.

"Well, I researched Tina Lindsay as well as everybody else, and of course, included in that was her husband, Brett. They have separated twice and filed for divorce, but both times they reconciled. There are a couple of allegations of domestic abuse by her. Evidently, she called 911 each time, and then when the officers came to their home, she said it was a mistake, and she wouldn't press charges."

"Wow, sounds like a volatile marriage," Kelly said.

"Not only that, but in one of the police reports, there is mention of her having a black eye and marks on her throat, as if someone had tried to strangle her."

"Lovely, Brett sounds like a real sweetheart."

"I'm not through, Kelly. Brett called 911 once because Tina was brandishing a gun and according to him, yelling that she was going to kill him. Neighbors confirmed that they heard the altercation and added that the reason she was going to kill him was because of his affairs."

"Well, that is interesting. So there's a history of violence as well as the possibility of him having affairs. Maybe she threatened to leave him, and he killed her. By chance, did you find anything out about their financial situation or life insurance, things of that nature?"

"They live in the home that Brett grew up in, his parents' home. I found no mortgage on it, so I assume with its age, they own it free and clear, or at least Brett does. I did see that her name was not on the title. As far as their bank account, they pretty much live from her paycheck to paycheck. As you mentioned, his income from the hardware store just barely pays to keep it open."

"Well, there may be a reason for him keeping it open."

"Oh?" Mike asked, and even though she couldn't see Mike, she knew him well enough to know that his eyebrows would be raised.

"I've heard that he likes the ladies, and when one of them goes into the hardware store, the open sign on the door is reversed to closed."

"Hmm," Mike said. "Taking this a step further, maybe this was a crime of passion by him. Maybe he found someone else and knew that Tina would never let him leave or divorce him. Any idea if he has any current lady friends, and if so, who they are?"

"No, but I have Liz working on that today. When we talked to Chris Jannette last night, he mentioned that he'd overheard a conversation in a local coffee shop between the cook and a waitress alluding to that. Liz is going to the coffee shop and hopefully, will be able to find out something. The coffee shop is right next door to Brett's hardware store."

"Good, that might get you somewhere. Now I've saved what I think may be your most valid suspect for last, Raquelle DuBois."

"I'm curious as to what you found, because Zoe had a sense that something was off with her," Kelly said.

"She might be right. Raquelle's had a couple of traffic tickets, but that's about the extent of her involvement with law enforcement. I don't know why, but I just had a feeling about her, maybe like Zoe's. I kept snooping and found out who she worked for prior to her job at the Hillside Resort."

"That was smart."

"I think it may bear fruit. She was at a company called

Bering Industries for several years. The company does multi-automotive things such as tow trucks, repairs, etc. They even have the county contract for towing. I didn't find out much there other than she was the bookkeeper.

"For some reason, I felt compelled to continue checking on it, so I went to the owner's website, Facebook page, and a number of social media sites he's active on. I also checked on his marital status. All of that."

"Thanks, Mike, I didn't think to do that last night. I just looked at her Facebook page and whatever I could find on social media."

"The man who owns Bering Industries is Jude Bering. He's forty years old and took over the company from his father, who wanted to retire to the Florida Keys and fish, which he did.

"Like most people, Jude has had several tickets and been involved in some court cases generally involving customers who didn't pay him. Small claims things. However, his wife filed for divorce a couple of years ago. Within two months, Raquelle DuBois left the company."

"That's interesting. I wonder if they were involved."

"I don't know. I didn't see anything about that. What I did see was a one-liner by him about that time saying he was never getting involved with an embezzler again," Mike said.

"What do you think that means?" Kelly asked.

"I have no idea, but it sure would be worth looking into."

"Yes, I agree. Do you know where he lives?"

"Kelly, please, give me some credit. Do you really think I would go to all this trouble knowing you'd want to talk to him without getting an address?"

"No, sorry. That was dumb of me to ask. What is it?"

Mike gave her the business address and the home address as well as telephone numbers for both. "I wonder if I should call or just go over there."

"Since you have a business address, I'd start there. I know it's Saturday, but a lot of automotive companies do their best business on Saturdays, and I'd be willing to bet he's working today."

"I'll call at 9:00, and I'd much rather go there than to his home and get involved with some new wife, particularly if he was having an affair with Raquelle."

"One last thing, Kelly, and then I know you have to go. I called Doc last night and invited him over here for dinner tonight. Liz must have called him because he knew all about the judge. He's really worried about Liz and the stress this has to be putting on her. I think it's a good thing you're keeping her busy today. Probably better if she doesn't have a lot of time to just sit and think."

"My sentiments exactly, Mike. I'll call you tonight and tell you what's happening. By the way, what are you cooking for Doc?"

"Silly woman. What would you cook for two men? Steak, baked potatoes with the trimmings, and a salad made with a package from the grocery store. I did take a cheesecake I found in the freezer out and put it in the refrigerator. Figure we can have that for dessert, and voila, a gourmet meal."

"Sounds great. Tell Doc not to worry, and that I'll make sure Liz is okay."

"I just thought of something else. If Liz is going to the Merritt Spa and the coffee shop, what are you going to do for a car?"

"When we were at the Jannettes late yesterday, they told me if I needed one to just call the valet desk. Chris said he would call and tell them I was to have one. Evidently the resort keeps several on hand for guests who fly in. I'll call them shortly."

"Good luck, sweetheart. I know you'll be successful."

"Thanks for your faith, Mike. Hope it's justified."

CHAPTER SIXTEEN

"Kelly, I called Cody Merritt, and I'm meeting him at 10:30 at his spa. Got any tips on how I should play this?" Liz asked as she walked into the living room where Kelly was eating a bagel and cream cheese she'd found in the refrigerator.

"Think of yourself as a reporter. What kind of questions would a reporter ask him about his spa? You could probably say that you'd heard he wanted to build a hotel on his property so he could create a destination resort people could come to while they're doing a wine tour of the area. I would also ask him if his spa differs from the Hillside Spa, and if so, how?"

"Okay, those are good suggestions. When I finish with him, I'll go to the coffee shop next to Brett's hardware store and see if I can find out anything there. Am I missing something?"

"No, that's all I can think of. Liz, when you're doing something like this, don't worry about it. Just be your normal, likeable self. You'll do fine."

"And what are you going to do today?" Liz asked.

"I'm just about to call Jude Bering. He's the head of Bering Industries and Raquelle DuBois used to work for him. Here's what Mike dug up last night," Kelly said as she relayed her conversation.

"That sounds very interesting. I wonder if he'll tell you what he meant by never getting involved with an embezzler again," Liz said.

"I have no idea, but if he's referring to Raquelle, it sure could put an interesting slant on things." She looked over at the clock on the stove and said, "Good, they should be open now. I'll go in my room and give him a call. Wish me luck."

"Fingers crossed," Liz said.

Kelly punched the numbers that Mike had given her into her cell phone and a moment later heard a young woman say, "Bering Industries, how may I direct your call?"

"I'd like to speak with Jude Bering. My name is Kelly Reynolds and this is a personal matter."

"Please hold, and I'll see if he's in."

A few moments later a deep male voice said, "This is Jude Bering. I understand that you wanted to speak to me regarding a personal matter. How can I help you?"

"Thanks for taking my call, Mr. Bering. I was hoping that you might have some free time this morning to talk to me. I'd prefer to discuss this in person, rather than on the phone."

"Let me check my calendar. I just walked into my office, so it will take a couple of minutes for my computer to warm up." He was quiet and then Kelly could hear the clicking of computer keys. "Actually, if you can get here soon, I'm free until 10:30, and then I have back-to-back appointments the rest of the day."

"I can be there in about fifteen minutes. I have your address and it looks like your office isn't that far from where I am."

"And that would be where?"

"I'm staying at the Hillside Resort."

"Good place to stay and no, it shouldn't take you more than fifteen minutes. I'll see you shortly," Jude said.

Kelly had called the valet desk earlier to request a car for the day. The person at the valet desk told her that Amy had called yesterday and left word that if Kelly needed a car, they were to provide one of the company cars for her.

She walked into the kitchen where Liz was eating breakfast and told her that she was on her way to see Jude Bering. Liz wished her luck and then Kelly rode down the elevator to the first floor to pick up her car.

As she got into it, she noticed that it was brand new, and it even had that smell that new cars have. She thanked the valet, tipped him, and left for Bering Industries.

Fifteen minutes later she pulled into Bering Industries parking lot and decided that she needed to talk to Mike about getting a new car. She hadn't realized just how old her car at home was and how wonderful it was to drive a car that had all the most up-to-date bells and whistles.

Kelly was well aware that she didn't know how to operate half of the things this car had on it, but she promised herself she'd learn when she got a new one. On the drive she'd fully convinced herself that she deserved it.

She walked into the large reception area and told the young man behind the desk that she was Kelly Reynolds and that she had an appointment with Jude Bering. He made a phone call and then said, "His office is down the hall. Third door on the left."

She knocked on the door that said, "Jude Bering, President," and was told to come in. She entered the room and a very attractive man, who looked to be in his 40's with black hair just beginning to get a bit silver at the temples, stood up and walked around his desk. "You must be Kelly Reynolds," he said putting out his hand. "I'm Jude Bering. Please, have a seat." She shook his hand and walked over to the chair he gestured to.

"Thanks for seeing me on such short notice," Kelly said. "I'm sure you're very busy, and I appreciate you taking the time to see me."

"Not a problem, but I must say your phone call certainly made me curious. What is this personal thing you want to talk to me about?" Jude asked.

"Jude, let me give you some background on why I'm here. I'm hoping that you'll understand the situation a little better when I finish." She told him about Liz, Zoe, the murder, and what Mike had told her the evening before. What she omitted was her absolute conviction that the judge in the case was Zoe's father. She still wasn't sure what she was going to do about that.

When she was finished, he looked at her and said, "Let me see if I understand where this is going, Kelly. You're curious if Raquelle's departure from Bering Industries and my divorce are tied in any way."

"Yes, and I would also like to know if the comment you made on social media about relationships and embezzlement had anything to do with that situation."

He looked away from Kelly and was quiet for several long moments, as if he was deliberating what to tell her. Finally, he said, "Yes, they are very much tied together. Here's what happened.

"I had an affair with Raquelle while I was married. Essentially the marriage was over except for going through the legal breakup. I know that's not an excuse, but I'm simply telling you so you can get a sense of where I was."

"Jude, you don't need to be concerned. I'm not judging you. People often have very valid reasons for what they do, and sometimes their actions are not exactly the way that society would dictate."

"Yes, I would certainly agree with that. Anyway, I came in the office one Sunday to get away from my wife. The only thing left for us to do was to hire an attorney because the marriage was dead, but neither one of us was anxious to take the first step. And I think we each were secretly hoping that maybe, just maybe, we could get our marriage back on track so we wouldn't have to take that step.

"Anyway, I realized I hadn't had a chance to look at the books for a long time, maybe a year. I'd just turned them over to Raquelle and trusted her to do them. Since we were having an affair, I naively assumed that she would never do something like embezzle funds from Bering Industries."

"I'm taking it that you found out that wasn't quite true," Kelly said.

"In spades. I spent several hours that day going over the books, and at the end of that time, I realized there was close to a $100,000 discrepancy. I didn't know whether I should go to the police or what I should do. I decided to go to Raquelle's house and confront her about it, which I did.

"I can't even imagine how betrayed you must have felt."

"Beyond. Anyway, I won't bore you with the details, but when I threatened Raquelle with me going to the police, she countered that she would go to my wife and tell her everything, even about the pictures."

Kelly looked at him with an unspoken question in her eyes.

"No, fortunately I wasn't stupid enough to do any nude photographs, but there were plenty of photographs on her cell phone, selfies of us, pictures of us kissing, hugging, and clearly involved in a romantic relationship. That would provide all the backup evidence my wife would need to divorce me."

"Sounds like she really put you in a bind," Kelly said.

"She did. The upshot was that we agreed I would not go to the police. I told Rachelle she would resign effective immediately for personal reasons and would not tell my wife about the affair. Yes, I lost a lot of money, but at the time I stupidly told myself that one couldn't select a price tag to put on their marriage, and that was just a price I had to pay."

"And then the marriage ended anyway," Kelly said. "How did you feel about it then?"

"Sorry I'd ever given Raquelle a good recommendation to Mrs. Jannette, and sorry I hadn't gone to the police. I've often wondered if she's embezzling from them. I thought about calling them, but then I decided not to get involved. Do you think she's been embezzling from them?" Jude asked.

"I have no idea, but given what happened to you, and the fact that she's handling the books, I think the odds are pretty good she is. But that still doesn't help me with Tina's murder. I'm not seeing a tie between the two," Kelly said.

"When you talked to Zoe, did she say that she'd told Raquelle she wanted to see the books?"

"No. She had an argument with Tina Lindsay the day of her murder about making all of the books and information available to her, because she felt that Tina had been stalling. However, she didn't say anything specifically about asking to see the accounting books and bank records Raquelle was handling."

"Well, have you considered the possibility that Raquelle and Tina may have been partnering in an embezzlement scheme, and neither one of them wanted Zoe to see the books?" Jude asked.

"No, that thought has never occurred to me. If that were so, I can see why Raquelle might have wanted to get rid of Tina because she knew, actually, was somewhat of a co-conspirator in the embezzling. However, that still doesn't explain why Raquelle would want to get rid of Zoe."

"It does if she was afraid Zoe would find out Raquelle had been embezzling from the spa."

Kelly sat back, trying to make sense of what she'd just learned from Jude. She looked at the clock on the wall and said, "You've been more than gracious in spending this much time with me, Jude, and I'll be leaving shortly, but I'd like to ask you one more question."

"Certainly. I don't seem to have any more secrets. What is it?"

"Do you think Raquelle is capable of committing murder?"

Jude was very quiet, spending a great deal of time flipping a pencil back and forth between his hands and looking intently at it. After a long pause he looked up at her and said, "Kelly, I honestly don't know. What I will say is that I had no idea when I was having the affair with Raquelle that she would be capable of embezzling funds from my company while, at the same time, I was having an affair with her.

"If she never had any qualms about doing that, than perhaps an extension of that thinking is yes, she could be capable of committing murder."

"I'm sorry, Jude, but this really will be my last question.

Do you have any idea of why she was embezzling?"

"Kelly, funny you should ask, because I've spent a lot of time thinking about that very same question. I'll tell you my different trains of thought. First of all, I wondered if she was doing it to help out her family or something like that, but then I remembered her telling me that she was an only child and both of her parents were deceased. Actually, I have to laugh about even thinking that she would be doing it for such an altruistic reason.

"Next I wondered if she was just doing it to get more money so she could spend more on glitzy stuff. Then I decided that wasn't it. She showed no signs of spending much money on herself, you know for things like jewelry, designer clothes, flashy cars. No, and trust me, after my last wife, I recognize the signs when a woman is spending a great deal of money on herself. She didn't even have her nails done or color her hair."

"And what did you finally decide?" Kelly asked.

"My last thought, and the only reason it stayed with me is because I discounted the others, is that she made several references to Mexico over the months we were involved. Evidently her mother was from Mexico, and Raquelle visited it with her a number of times when she was young. She spoke about it in almost reverential tones, and I know she was fluent in Spanish because I heard her speak it several times to people. I wonder if she was embezzling to earn enough money to move there permanently?"

"Interesting," Kelly said. "I have no idea and probably never will. Again, Jude, thank you for your time and trusting me with your confidences. I don't know where this is going, but at least I feel like I know a little more about the woman. If you think of something, I'd appreciate it if you'd call me. Here's my card with my cell number on it."

"Nice meeting you Kelly. And in the same vein, if you do find something out, I'd appreciate it if you'd give me a call," Jude said.

"I will. Thanks again," Kelly said as she walked out the door.

When she got in her car, she decided to call Finn and bring him up to date on what Mike had found out and her meeting with Jude. When she'd finished telling him, he said, "Kelly, you're amazing. I wish I didn't have to practice law and could just devote my time to solving this case."

"Finn, based on what Jude told me, is there any way we can use that to discredit Raquelle's statement about seeing Zoe leave the jacuzzi?"

He was quiet for a few minutes and then said, "I wish we could, because I certainly think it's valid. Here's the problem. From what you told me Jude did not pursue the embezzlement. He never went to the police so there really is no record of Raquelle ever being charged with embezzlement.

"It would become a liar's contest, his word against hers, and that's assuming he'd even agree to go public with it. From what I understand, he told you about it somewhat in confidence. I don't think it's something he would want his employees or customers to know about. It kind of puts a dark cloud over his business management skills. And I don't know what the financial arrangements are with his company, but if he has stockholders, they sure wouldn't want to hear something like that."

"I hadn't thought about that. Finn, I really am beginning to wonder if Raquelle is embezzling from the spa, and the murder and the accusations against Zoe are a coverup for it."

"It could be, but I also wonder if Tina was in on it and they had a falling out? Maybe Raquelle had been putting pressure on Tina not to let Zoe look at the records, because she was sure Zoe would find out what either she was doing or what she and Tina were doing together," Finn said.

"And the way to find that out would be how?" Kelly asked.

"I would think if you could get the bookkeeping records and you had someone who knew something about accounting take a look at them, that would let us know whether or not she's embezzling. However, that would be difficult to do. If she is embezzling, she wouldn't want anyone to take a look at them."

"Finn, I'm very good with numbers. It's kind of an innate talent of mine. When I was in high school, I started doing my parents' taxes, and I've always done mine since, as well as my coffee shop. In fact, my husband kids me and says that if the coffee shop fails, I can always get a job as a bookkeeper."

"Well, that would be great, and I have a background in it, too, which I won't bore you with now. The problem is getting the books. I would imagine the door to Raquelle's office would be locked, and we certainly don't want you arrested for breaking and entering. Think about it, and I will too. Maybe we can come up with an idea."

"I'm pretty sure I can get in there, Finn. I'll get back to you later."

"I'll be waiting for your call."

CHAPTER SEVENTEEN

Liz drove into the parking lot of the Merritt Spa and thought how visually eye-appealing it was. She had to give Cody Merritt credit for having the courage to build it in a Mediterranean style, which was quite different from other buildings in the area which were designed in a more traditional Pacific Northwest wood style. She wondered if he was deliberately trying to give people a totally different experience from the Hillside Spa.

She parked and went in. On the left was a shop filled with various kinds of face and body lotions as well as all things associated with spas. There was even a wine section, highlighting the pinot noirs, for which this region was famous.

The reception desk was curved, and there were two beautiful young women sitting behind it with computers in front of them. She assumed that the women had been hired for their good looks, the subtle message to the spa guest being that if you come to this spa, you, too, can look like this.

"May I help you?" the beautiful young women with the name tag, MacKenzie, on her white silk blouse asked.

"Yes. My name is Liz Burkham, and I have an appointment with Cody Merritt."

"Certainly, Mrs. Burkham. Please follow me." She walked over to an oval wrought-iron staircase and began climbing up the stairs, Liz behind her. When they got to the second floor, MacKenzie motioned towards a long hallway and said, "The offices are on both sides of the hallway, and Mr. Merritt's is the last one on the right."

"Thank you," Liz said. She walked down the hall on the tile floor, the Mediterranean theme being followed in the décor of the inside of the building as well. The door to his office was open, but she knocked before going in.

The man Liz assumed was Cody Merritt was sitting at a desk peering intently at the computer in front of him. He looked like what she'd picture the owner of a spa would look like with his perfectly groomed hair and nails that were so polished, he must have recently had a manicure. He was dressed casually in a blue denim shirt and jeans with boots, but the shirt and jeans had been carefully ironed, and the boots were highly polished.

When she knocked, he looked up, smiled, and said, "You must be Liz Burkham. Please have a seat. May I get you some coffee or water?"

"No, thanks. First of all, I really appreciate you taking the time to see me. I'm writing an article on this area of Oregon, and since there have already been so many articles done on the different wineries here, I thought I would do something different. I want to highlight the spas of this area."

"I think that's a great idea. Something people can do in addition to, or instead of, wine tasting. What would you like from me?" Cody asked.

"First of all, your permission to let me record this. I've found I do much better if I record my interviews, because I often get so wrapped up in what we're talking about, I tend to leave out the details. Would that be all right with you?" she asked.

"I have no problem with that," Cody said.

"Great." Liz took a small recorder out of her purse and turned it on. It was the same recorder she used in her psychology treatment sessions with patients. "There. Okay, now we can start. Here are some things I'm interested in. How is the spa industry doing, not just your spa, but the general industry? What do you see as the future of spas in the area? What is your relationship with the Hillside Spa? From what my research indicated, I think you two are the largest spas in the area."

"Certainly. The spa industry is doing well," Cody said. "I know that the country is in a bit of a recession, but interestingly enough, people don't seem to mind spending money on feeling and looking good. I've often thought that in times of financial stress, people think if they look and feel good, they can weather whatever they have to deal with."

"That's a very astute observation, Mr. Merritt," Liz said.

"Thank you. We're operating here pretty much at maximum capacity. One thing I have noticed in the last couple of years is that we're seeing more men coming here for treatments. It seems that the stigma of men doing things for their bodies, or even having facials and pedicures, has dramatically decreased in recent years.

"As a result, I've added a number of special treatments just for men. As far as the future of the spa business goes, I feel that people have come to believe they need to take care of themselves, and I think the spa business has profited from that feeling and will continue to," Cody said.

"With that in mind, do you think you'll be enlarging the Merritt Spa?" Liz asked.

"I would very much like to. I have been in talks for the last couple of years with developers to build a hotel on this property, so that it would become a destination resort. Unfortunately, in times like these, developers are very hesitant to take on something like that in a remote area, which this essentially is.

"As a matter of fact, I just returned to the spa last night after spending three days in Los Angeles meeting with a developer by the name of Robert Campbell of RC Industries. You've probably heard of them if you've done much research on spas. They've built a lot of the major ones in areas known for their spas like Arizona, New Mexico, and California.

"He likes the Mediterranean theme I've used for the spa and agrees with me that people seem to relate to that style of architecture for resorts and spas. He's quite interested in my proposal, and I really hope it works out."

"For your sake, I hope it does too. What about your relationship with the Hillside Spa and the resort?"

"I would say that we have a good relationship. Obviously, we're competitors, but friendly. I've even asked them if we could do some sort of merger, but they don't feel that's something they want to get involved in. They feel that with the Hillside Resort having its spa, hotel, and vineyards all in one place, it would be jarring to have a satellite spa in another area.

"I would have liked to have done that, because it would be good advertising for me, but I understand their point of view. I'm on what I would consider good terms with Amy and Chris Jannette, the owners. Although I really feel for them with their daughter being charged with the murder of one of their employees."

"Yes, I agree. It's a tragedy. They seem like very nice people, and this has to be a horrible thing for them to go through. Did you know the decedent?"

"I'd met her a couple of times at various events, but I can't say I really knew her. Some of my employees work part-time for me and part-time for the Hillside Spa, and from time to time, they tell me things," Cody said.

"Care to share any of those? I'll make sure it's off the record and even turn off my recorder," Liz said.

"I really don't like to gossip, but now that she's deceased, I suppose it doesn't matter. A lot of people didn't like Tina. What I heard was that she and her assistant, a woman by the name of Raquelle DuBois, had some sort of weird relationship.

"After Tina turned the bookkeeping for the spa over to Raquelle, so she could concentrate on internet marketing, several employees complained that they were paid incorrect amounts when they got their paychecks.

"They mentioned that it had never happened when Tina was doing the books, but with Raquelle, there always seemed to be something off."

"What kind of things, Cody?"

"One thing I heard several times is that they weren't being paid their commission on retail things that had been sold in the shop at the spa. As a little background, when an employee performs a treatment, whether it's a facial or a massage, or whatever, they use certain products. When a guest's treatment is complete, the guest is given a little card telling them which products were used during the treatment.

"Probably something like 65% of the guests purchase those products and the person conducting the treatment gets paid a percentage of the sale price as a commission. It's a win-win situation. The spa makes money, the person giving the treatment makes money, and the guests get the products they want."

"So what you've heard is that there have been some glitches in that area," Liz said.

"Yes, and I've often thought it happened too many times to be accidental. I'm not accusing anyone of anything, but if the person who handled the books wanted to skim a little, that would be an easy way to do it. The spa shop sells the products and credits the treatment person in the transaction. However, unless the person who sold the products in the spa shop tells the aesthetician or whomever, or their customer tells them, they'll never know the guest bought something."

"Interesting. Have you ever had a problem here with that?" Liz asked.

"No, but I have all my aestheticians and those who perform services fill out the customer product lists they give the customers in duplicate. They keep a copy, and when their client checks out and buys products, they receive a copy of the client's receipt, showing what products they bought. That way they can very easily check it against what their paycheck shows for product sales," Cody said.

"So if someone wanted to say, fudge on the books, that's one way they could."

"Yes, but if someone really wanted to get serious about it, and there was very little oversight, there are a number of other ways they could as well."

"How do you get around that?" Liz asked.

"I go over the books at least three times a week. I oversee the products that are bought, I examine the records for spa appointments, and carefully check the bookkeeping entries. Additionally, I have told my entire staff, that if there are any errors in paychecks or anything else financial, to come to me, and it will remain confidential. I can say pretty confidently that hasn't happened here."

"Cody, if you had heard some talk that a little skimming

might be going on at the Hillside Spa, and you're on friendly terms with the Jannettes, why didn't you say something to them?"

He was quiet for several moments and then said, "For the same reason parents resent people who tell them how to raise their children. I had no proof, and quite frankly, to say something like that to someone implies that you think they're not managing whatever the way they should.

"I have a good relationship with them, and I knew that would probably ruin it. In retrospect, considering there's been a death at the spa, a death their daughter is accused of being responsible for, I wish I had. As I said, I've met Zoe, and I have no doubt that she is incapable of murder. This is a tragedy, and I certainly hope that the truth will come out about it before it's too late."

So do I, Liz thought. *Cody, you have no idea how much I hope that.*

"Cody, you've been more than generous with your time, and I appreciate that. I work freelance, so once I've written the article and submitted it to several publishers, I may want to come back and get more photographs. I took some of the outside of your spa before I came in. Again, thanks for seeing me. I learned a lot."

Liz stood up and walked over to the door. "Good luck with the article. Let me know if you need anything else," Cody said as he joined her and shook her hand. "Drive safely."

As Liz smiled and walked away, she thought *Way to go, Elizabeth, you rookie investigator. You just hit a home run!*

CHAPTER EIGHTEEN

On the drive back to the coffee shop, Liz thought about what Cody had told her. It seemed that a lot of the pieces of the puzzle were beginning to fall into place. While she was sorry that Cody hadn't spoken to Amy or Chris about his suspicions, she understood his reasons for not doing so. It would be somewhat like her trying to give them advice on how to raise Zoe. Definitely not politically correct!

When she walked into the coffeeshop and immediately thought she was in a time warp. It looked like something out of a 1950's movie. The booths were red vinyl, there was a jukebox in the corner, red vinyl covered the round stools at the counter and the waitress was wearing a pink and white striped outfit with a hat to match.

"Sit anywhere ya' want, darlin'," a voice said, peering out from the kitchen. "Slow this time of day, so ya' got yer choice. Be with ya' in a minute."

Liz walked over and sat down at a booth by the window which had a clear view of the Lindsay Hardware store. She was hoping that the woman who had just spoken to her was the waitress that Chris had overheard.

A few minutes later an overweight bleached blond waitress, who was chewing gum and looked like her "use by this date" label had expired long ago, walked over to her and asked if Liz would like some coffee while she looked over the menu. She replied yes.

"Here ya' go, honey," the waitress wearing the name badge of Maisie said when she returned with Liz's coffee. What can I get ya' to eat?"

"Nothing at the moment. Let me drink this cup of coffee and think about it. I'm just kind of biding my time until the hardware store opens. I see it has a closed sign on the front door, but I thought for sure it would be open on a Saturday," Liz said.

"Yeah, ya'd think, wouldn't ya'? But gotta tell ya, gal, nothin' that Brett guy does surprises me. I've seen him turn the open sign to closed more times than I can count," Maisie harumphed.

"That seems strange. I would think in a town this small, he'd want to get as many customers in there as he could."

"Customers ain't what's uppermost on his mind. Guy's got one thing on his mind, if ya' know what I mean." She looked around to see if anyone was listening, and then she said, "If it wears a skirt and looks interestin' to him, ya' can bet that sign'll be turned to closed faster than ya' can say Lindsay Hardware."

"Well, that's something," Liz said. "So you think he likes the ladies?"

"Nah, I don't think that, I know it. But he mighta' found one that likes him jes' as much. Leastways, she's been a real regular fer the last couple of months."

"Isn't he, or should I say, wasn't he married? I think I heard something on the news that his wife was recently murdered. Maybe that's why the store isn't open. Maybe he's in mourning," Liz said.

"Darlin', if ya' believe that, bet ya' still put a stockin' up for Santa every Christmas, expectin' him to fill it 'cuz yer' a good girl," Maisie said. "Jes' between us, I think he and his latest flavor of the month, or should I say months, had somethin' to do with it. Don't add up in my book."

"What makes you say that?" Liz asked.

Maisie looked around again and then said in a conspiratorial voice, "Well, I was parkin' my car behind the coffee shop here a few days ago, and I heard some loud voices comin' from his store. Couldn't help myself, jes' had to hear what all the yellin' was 'bout."

"I don't blame you," Liz said. "I would have done the same. This sounds like a soap opera. What did you hear?"

"I heard him, Brett, tellin' someone, a woman, that he couldn't do it. She'd have to do it. And then he said he didn't know that Tina, that's his wife, was takin' money from the spa." Maisie looked at Liz to see what her reaction was.

"Good grief. That's embezzling. I think I remember that his wife worked for the spa. Do you think she was doing something like that?"

Maisie nodded her head. "Yep. And ya' wanna' hear the worst of it?"

"Please, don't leave me hanging. What did the woman say?"

"She said she'd take care of Tina and make it all look like it was the daughter of the owners who dun' it. Said she'd never get caught, and after one more month, she and Brett could go to Mexico, jes' like they'd been plannin' on doin', but she needed a little more money."

"Wow, Maisie. That's quite a story."

"Ain't no story. That's what I heard," she said nodding her head up and down.

"Since Tina was murdered and the owners' daughter was arrested for the murder, are you going to tell the sheriff what you heard?"

She was quiet for a few moments, and then said. "Nah. I'm old, and a lot of people think I'm losin' it, if ya' know what I mean. Plus, never saw the woman. Jes' heard her voice. Don't think the sheriff would do nothin' 'cuz I ain't got no eyeball evidence."

"Well, that's true, but still... I would think he'd be interested in hearing something like that."

"Sweet cheeks, ya' jes' don't know Sheriff Kuyper. Guy never had a grey day in his life. To him, everything's either black or its white. Nothin' in between. Kind of a sad way to live if ya' ask me, jes' lookin' fer the black in everybody."

"Yes, I see what you mean. Just the fact you overheard

that conversation probably wouldn't hold up in court. I suppose the sheriff would want some kind of stronger evidence."

"Yeah, and now that I think 'bout it, didn't see the hardware store open yesterday, either. Maybe he's decided not to work no more. Maybe he had some big life insurance policy on his wife. Wouldn't that beat all?"

"That it would. Maisie, it's been nice talking to you. Think I might as well take off since it looks like the hardware store won't be opening today. Hope to see you soon."

"Yeah, and I don't want ya' to be blabbin' to anyone 'bout the conversation we jes' had," Maisie said, as she looked over to the door where a couple had just walked in.

"What conversation, Maisie?" Liz said with a wink as she put a five-dollar bill on the table and headed to the door.

CHAPTER NINETEEN

"Oh, Kelly, I'm so glad you're here. I have so much to tell you," Liz blurted out when she walked into the suite.

"And I have just as much to tell you, but let's wait for a little while. Finn is on his way over here, and there's no sense for each of us to have to repeat it. I need to call Amy and talk to her. I just had some lunch, so why don't you make yourself something to eat while I'm on the phone with Amy?"

"Sounds good. I was thinking of having something at the coffee shop, but by the time I finished talking to the waitress, I figured I might as well get back here."

"I take it from that," Kelly said, "that your morning outing was a success."

"Yes, on both fronts."

"Good, I'll be back in a few minutes. If Finn knocks on the door, let him in."

Kelly walked into her bedroom and called Amy. "This is

Amy Jannette, how may I help you?"

"Amy, it's Kelly. I've found out some things about Raquelle DuBois that are quite disturbing. I think she's been embezzling funds from the spa. I won't go into the full conversation with you, but here's what I learned from her previous employer, Jude Bering."

"How can that be, Kelly? He gave her a fantastic reference."

"To keep things brief, I won't go into the whole background on it now. Suffice it to say it was kind of if you keep your mouth shut, I'll keep my mouth shut."

"Oh no! What changed?" Amy asked.

"His wife divorced him, and he felt that he was no longer bound by the agreement he'd made with Raquelle."

"I don't quite understand it, but I think I'm getting the picture. And you think she may be involved in Tina's murder and Zoe's arrest?"

"I do, but I don't have enough hard evidence yet to take it to the sheriff. As a matter of fact, I don't have any hard evidence, and that's why I'm calling you. I'm assuming you have a key to Raquelle's office as well as one to her desk."

"Yes, I do. Why?"

"I'm very good with accounting, numbers and things like that. I want to go over the spa's financial records and see if there are any discrepancies, but I'd like you to be with me. Does Raquelle work Saturday afternoons?"

"No. She works Saturday morning, and then she's off Saturday afternoon and Sunday. She has Tuesday afternoons off as well, because that's the spa's slowest day. Why don't you come to the house at say, 3:00 this afternoon, and fill me in on everything? We can walk over to the spa from the house."

"That will work well. Liz had a couple of appointments this morning, and I just saw her briefly, but I haven't really had a chance to talk to her. She told me that she'd found out a lot as well. Finn, Zoe's public defender, is coming over here shortly. I want him to be in the loop on everything and advise us what to do legally with what we've found out."

"Kelly, so much has happened I can't remember if I ever properly thanked you for dropping everything to come here and help us. I just want you to know how appreciative Chris and I are."

"Amy, I want nothing more than to see your daughter cleared of these charges. I have a feeling we're getting close to doing that. With any luck she'll be out of jail shortly. See you this afternoon."

Kelly walked into the living room and found Finn and Liz talking. "Finn, it's good to see you. I wanted you to come here so Liz and I both could tell you what we've found out this morning. We haven't had a chance to talk to each other, so what we're about to tell you will be the first time the other one has heard it. If you don't mind, I'll go first."

She told him what Mike had found out regarding Jude Bering and her meeting with him this morning. "He was very open with me, feeling that his and Raquelle's past agreement didn't matter since his wife had divorced him. He discovered that Raquelle had embezzled a substantial amount from his company."

"Did he go to the sheriff about it?" Finn asked.

"No, for one thing, I think he felt like a fool, and secondly, he and Raquelle made an agreement, that at the time, seemed the right thing for him to do in order to keep his marriage from ending. She wouldn't tell his wife about their affair in return for him not turning her in for embezzlement."

"Sounds like he made a deal with the devil," Finn said.

"I think now he'd agree with you, but at the time it sounded like a good way for each of them to escape from a bad situation."

"Okay, Kelly, I'm assuming that what you're thinking is that if Raquelle did it once, she could easily do it again. But that doesn't link her to Tina's murder. I don't see any tie-in between the two."

"I think I can shed some light on that," Liz said. She told them about her conversation with Maisie and what she'd overheard. "If Raquelle was the one embezzling, and she was paying something to Tina because she'd helped her, Raquelle may have wanted to get rid of her. More money for her."

"Liz, did Maisie see the woman who was talking to Brett?" Finn asked.

"No, and that's why she didn't go to the sheriff. She had

nothing solid. Just something she overheard, and there could be nothing to it, but the more I think about it, I'd bet Raquelle and Brett were having an affair. Maybe they acted together. Kill Tina, and Raquelle could get more money, and Brett could get his hands on the money that Tina had been paid by Raquelle."

Finn was quiet for a few moments and then he said, "Not a bad theory, but still not enough for me to go to Sheriff Kuyper with and get the charges against Zoe dismissed. By the way, I stopped by to see her on my way here."

"How's she doing?" Liz asked.

"As well as could be expected. My heart goes out to her. We talked for a while, and she could add nothing to our conversation of yesterday. I wish there was something I could do for her. It sounds to me like she is simply an innocent victim. At least I was able to get her to smile once, so I considered that a win."

Hmm, Kelly thought, *sounds to me like he's doing more for her than would be required. Wonder if we're looking at the beginning of something. Wouldn't that be interesting? That she had to be charged with murder to meet him.*

"I would think you would," Kelly said. She turned towards Liz and said, "Liz, why don't you fill us in on your morning meetings? I believe we have the gist of what happened at the coffee shop, but how was Cody Merritt?"

"I liked him a lot, and I kind of feel guilty that I had to use the ploy that I was writing an article about the spas in the area, however I did leave myself an out. I told him I was a freelancer, so I'd see if I could get it published. Hopefully, when he doesn't hear back from me, he'll think it was because I couldn't."

"Yes, I agree," Kelly said. "I've had to do a few things over the years that I've cringed a bit about later on. However, I think this is one of those cases where the ends justify the means. So, fill us in."

"I can do better than that. I recorded our conversation, so you could listen. Since I've never done anything quite like this, I didn't want to rely on my memory or notes." She turned on her small recorder, and they listened to her conversation.

"I think he was very upfront and honest with you. If anything, it just points to Raquelle embezzling funds from the spa. He practically gave you a blueprint for some ways it could be done.

"I called Amy," Kelly continued, "and I'm meeting with her at her house at 3:00 this afternoon to fill her in on what we both learned today. After that she's going to accompany me to the spa. She has keys to Raquelle's office and her desk. I want to look over the books. I'm pretty good with figures and think I can get a sense if Raquelle, was in fact, embezzling."

"Kelly," Finn said, I'd like to go with you. My undergraduate degree was in accounting, so I'll know if figures are making sense or not. As a matter of fact, during college and law school, I worked at an accounting firm in order to help pay for my education expenses. I think between us, and what Cody told Liz, we should be able to determine if there are problems with the spa's books."

"Great, between you, Amy, and me, we should get some kind of a feel if she's been embezzling. Finn, if we determine that she has, what happens then?"

"I'll go to the sheriff and show him what we've come up with. I would tell him that this casts an aspersion on Raquelle's character as well as her statement that she saw Zoe coming out of the jacuzzi. Since Zoe was going to be examining the books, I think that provides a good motive for Raquelle to want Zoe out of the picture.

"That sounds good. With three of us doing this, it should give weight to the fact that we think she's embezzling. However, something just occurred to me. If Tina was in on this, and from what Liz found out from Maisie, there is certainly a good reason to think so, maybe there would be something in her desk that would indicate she was being paid by Raquelle."

"I think we absolutely should look in it. I'm assuming that Amy has keys to Tina's office and desk as well," Finn said.

"I'm sure she does. Before we leave, I want to get a little more comfortable. I'll be back in a minute and then I think we should head for Amy's," Kelly said. "Liz, we'll count on you to hold down the fort."

"I can do that. Anything else you need from me?" Liz asked.

"Can't think of anything. Why don't you treat this time as a bit of break for you?" Kelly asked.

A few minutes later, Kelly returned from her bedroom

wearing jeans and a tee-shirt. "I have no idea how long this will take, but at least I'll be comfortable. Are you ready, Finn?"

"Let's do it. The sooner we find something, the sooner we can get Zoe out of jail."

"I like the way you think, Finn," Liz said with a grin.

CHAPTER TWENTY

Kelly and Finn rode the elevator down to the first floor and then walked along the pathway that led to the Jannette's home. Kelly knocked on the door and moments later, it was opened by Chris.

"Please come in," he said, "Amy will be here any minute. She walked over to the spa to see what was happening. Come in and have a seat."

Niko was standing by Chris and immediately walked over to Kelly, nuzzling her hand. Then he went over to Finn, who held his hand out to the big dog. Satisfied that he was okay, Niko laid down at Kelly's feet after she sat down in the chair Chris had indicated.

Kelly was just getting ready to introduce Finn to Chris when the door opened and Amy walked in. "Amy, Chris, I'd like you to meet Finn O'Conner. Finn is Zoe's public defender. He wanted to accompany us to the spa, Amy, because he's very knowledgeable about accounting."

They shook hands and then Amy said, "Kelly, Finn, I'm really nervous about this. Accounting is not my strong suit, and if Raquelle has been embezzling, then it's my fault. Because I don't like dealing with numbers, I haven't been as diligent in that area as I should have been.

"As a matter of fact, that's one of the reasons I was really looking forward to Zoe getting involved in the business. She has a business mind and is really good with figures. My strength for the spa was more in having it be as state-of-the-art as it could be as far as the types of treatments and products that were offered."

"Amy, don't worry about it. When Liz met with Cody Merritt earlier today, she learned a lot about how one could do what we think Raquelle was doing.

"Before we go to the spa, I want to go over with you what Liz and I learned today and why I feel that Raquelle has been embezzling from the spa." Kelly spent the next twenty minutes filling them in on what they'd learned.

"And you think there's a very good chance that Tina was getting money from Raquelle. In other words, they'd been in on it together, and I was the one who really pushed the whole thing over the edge when I asked Tina to turn the books over to Raquelle," Amy said. "If that's true, then I'm indirectly to blame for Zoe being charged with murder."

"You can't think that way, Amy," Kelly said. "We have no way of knowing if Tina and Raquelle had been doing this when Tina was primarily in charge of the books. This may have been going on for a long time and Raquelle just got a little greedier and wanted Tina out of the way."

"Amy," Finn said. "Raquelle probably felt she was under a lot of pressure to never let Zoe examine the books. And if Tina was out of the way and Zoe was in jail, or even prison, she could continue embezzling for as long as she wanted. She had everything to gain with those two being out of the way. It really makes perfect sense.

"When we go over to the spa, why don't I examine the appointment records and calculate what should have been brought in by them. Why don't one of you handle the products and the other one look at the overall picture? If you have a better way to do it, I'm certainly open to any suggestions," Amy said.

"Finn, you're the one with the strong accounting background. Why don't you be the one to look at the overall picture. I'll take the products. Sound good?" Kelly said.

"Sure, but I'm assuming that everything is computerized," Finn said. "I would suggest that one of us sit in Tina's office and use her computer. I need her password to get in."

"Not a problem," Amy said. "I have the passwords to both of their computers. The offices are side by side, and there are only two chairs in Raquelle's office. It would be tight with three of us in there, plus it would take a lot more time. This will work out great because, Kelly, you're going to need the pricing sheets for the products which are contained in a loose-leaf binder.

"The companies send us their bills and once you've gotten a sense of that, we can check it against the computer records. Actually, this may go a lot easier than I'd thought. Are you ready?"

"Yes, is the spa usually busy on a late Saturday afternoon?" Kelly asked.

"No. It's actually very quiet. I'll be surprised if there are more than one or two treatments being conducted right now. We'll go in the back door. I don't want to draw any unnecessary attention to us. Plus, I want to bring Nico with us. I know it sounds crazy, but as I told Liz, he's a trained guard dog, and if we run into any problems, it would make me feel a lot more comfortable to have him around.

"Amy, I can't tell you how many times my guard dog has saved my life in situations where I never expected anything to happen. By all means, bring him along," Kelly said, standing up. Later, Kelly would well remember those words.

CHAPTER TWENTY-ONE

Amy unlocked the back door of the spa and the four of them walked down the silent hall to the two offices that had been used by Tina and Raquelle. Amy motioned Finn into the office used by Tina and said, "I wrote down her password. Here it is," she said as she handed him a piece of paper.

"The overall books are in the file marked Hillside Spa Ledger. And here's the key to her desk. We'll be in the room next to you. Please close the door so we don't disturb any of the spa guests."

Finn easily found the file and began to familiarize himself with the setup of the books, which were not all that different from most corporate records. He spent an hour making notes to himself, copying items and forwarding them to his own email, and from time to time shook his head. From what he was seeing, there was no doubt someone had embezzled funds from the spa, and the amount was staggering.

After a cursory look at the records, he began to search

Tina's desk. In the third drawer he looked in, he found a file marked "From Raquelle." In it were monthly records of how much Raquelle had embezzled and the amounts that she'd paid Tina. Finn did some quick math in his head and came up with a figure of over $200,000.

He locked the desk and the door to the office and went next door. "Kelly, Amy, how are you doing?" he asked, closing the door behind him and leaning against the wall.

"We've been talking while we've been working," Amy said as she idly reached down and petted Niko who was sleeping under the desk, "and there is no doubt in my mind that the amounts shown in the computer for the net income generated by spa appointments is way under what it should be. There's a huge discrepancy in the figures."

Finn looked at Kelly and said, "How do the products look?"

"Like someone has tampered with these figures. They simply don't match up. No wonder so many of the aestheticians and spa people have been concerned they weren't getting paid the commissions they were entitled to on the products that were sold. And the problem is there is no clear record of whether or not they've been accurately paid for the products. There's really no way to know."

"How would we fix that?" Amy asked.

"Cody told Liz what he did, and I'll tell you about it later. It's very doable. Cody is very knowledgeable about making sure that nothing like that happens. You might want to talk to him after this is over. And you, Finn, any luck?" Kelly asked.

"Bonanza luck. There is no doubt in my mind that Raquelle has been embezzling funds from the spa, and I'd say my rough estimate is it's around $200,000."

Upon hearing those words, Amy gasped. "Oh no, I don't believe it. How could that happen?"

"I don't know, but at least we found out, and now you can take steps to make sure it never happens again," Finn said. "And keep in mind that's just a quick look. I also found something that I think is the most damning."

"What's that?" Kelly asked.

"I found a folder, the one I have here, marked 'From Raquelle'. In it are the monthly amounts that Raquelle paid Tina. I want to show it to the sheriff and have her arrested not only for embezzlement, but for the murder of Tina Lindsay. Based on what we found, I would think we could get Zoe released from jail and the charges dropped in a matter of hours."

At that moment the door opened and the three of them turned towards it and saw a woman holding a gun in her hand. She quietly closed the door behind her. "Raquelle, what are you doing here?" Amy asked.

Kelly slowly moved her hand into her purse and clicked the record button on her phone, then slowly withdrew it. Raquelle was so focused on Amy and the file folder that Finn was holding, she didn't notice Kelly's movement.

"Well, since this is my office," Raquelle said, "it's rather obvious. I came here to pick up a few things, and I overheard your conversation. I'm not going to kill you here, because there are people in the building, but there's a lovely forest just beyond the spa that would be a perfect place for bodies to be hidden. Bodies that won't be discovered for several months or years. It really doesn't matter, because I've already decided to leave tonight."

Unbeknownst to Raquelle, Niko had quietly crept out of the small area where he'd been sleeping under the desk and had moved around to the far side of the desk, which was blocked from Raquelle's view.

"We're going to leave now," Raquelle said. "I want you to walk out into the hall and go to the back door. Open it and start walking towards the forest. I have my gun on you, and trust me, I will shoot to kill. All you need for verification is to remember what I did to Tina Lindsay. Shot her at point blank range three times in the chest while she was lounging in the jacuzzi."

The three of them started to edge towards the door, Raquelle standing off to the side. As they reached the door, Niko jumped out from his hidden position behind the desk and lunged at Raquelle, knocking her to the floor and causing her gun to go off, firing a bullet harmlessly into the ceiling. Niko placed his big paws firmly on Raquelle's chest and pinned her to the floor.

By the time Niko had Raquelle motionless on the floor, Finn had drawn his gun from a shoulder holster and had it trained on Raquelle. Kelly reached down and picked up Raquelle's gun.

"Finn, call the sheriff. I've handled plenty of guns. As a matter of fact my husband is a sheriff, so I'll keep Raquelle covered while you call him," Kelly said.

Within a matter of minutes, the sheriff arrived, joined by several of his deputies. Fortunately, he'd been in the area and within a short period of time, Raquelle had been read her rights and taken to a waiting sheriff's car by two deputies, headed to jail for the murder of Tina Lindsay and the attempted murder of Amy, Kelly, and Finn.

Finn was the one who did most of the talking. He related to the sheriff the details about the embezzlement, the records they'd found regarding the bookkeeping discrepancies, and he showed the sheriff the folder he'd found in Tina's desk.

"Sheriff, you also might be interested in this. When Raquelle walked in here, I started to record her on my phone. I'd like you to hear her words." Kelly played the tape for him.

"Mrs. Reynolds, would you send that tape to me? I'm sure the District Attorney can make use of it." He turned to Finn and said, "As of this moment, I'm dropping all charges against Zoe Jannette. Would one of you like to come to the jail and pick her up? I'm on my way there. I need to do the paperwork both for her release and write up the charges against Raquelle."

"I'll go and get her," Finn said. Then he turned toward Amy and said, "If that's alright with you."

"Yes, that would be fine. I'm shaking so much I doubt that I could drive, anyway. And I need to tell Chris about everything. Obviously, we're going to have to make some internal changes to the way the spa has been operated."

"With Zoe out of jail, she should probably be the one to

handle it. I suppose that might be called a type of baptism by fire." Kelly said.

"I agree," Amy said. "I don't know about you, Kelly, but I could sure use a glass of wine about now. And Finn, I'll have one waiting for you and Zoe when you get back here to the resort. Just come straight to the house."

"Sounds great," Kelly said, "but if you don't mind, I'd like to invite Liz to join us. I'm sure she's been on pins and needles waiting for Finn and me to return."

"Absolutely. For the first time in quite a while, we have something major to celebrate. And I think Zoe would like to meet Liz. Do you think that will be a problem for Liz? It just seems like the right thing to do at this time."

"I'll ask her, but I doubt it," Kelly said.

CHAPTER TWENTY-TWO

"Liz is on her way, and she can't wait to meet Zoe. Are you sure it will be alright with Zoe?" Kelly asked worriedly after Amy had filled Chris in on what had happened.

"Absolutely, she's always told us that if she ever had the chance, she'd like to meet her biological parents. And really, Kelly, there never has been an issue about her adoption. She knows how much we love her, and she feels the same way about us, plus she's always told us how grateful she is that we're her parents.

"She also has said on numerous occasions that she's glad her biological parents cared enough about her future to give her to us for adoption. I know that her birth father isn't listed on her birth certificate, but I'm sure there were good reasons for that. Maybe someday she can find out who he is and complete her family tree."

"How would you and Chris feel about meeting her birth father?" Kelly asked.

"Absolutely fine. We'd just be happy for Zoe, because it would be a form of completion for her. We harbor absolutely no ill feelings towards him. I wish there were a way to find out who he is, but I don't think that's possible.

Maybe there is, Kelly thought, *and I'm definitely going to try. I just need to do a few things, and then I think I can make it happen.*

Amy poured them all a glass of the Hillside Resort's premium wine and they toasted Zoe's release. A moment later there was a knock on the door. Chris walked over and opened it for Liz.

"Come in, come in. We're just toasting Zoe's release. Please join us. Zoe and Finn should be here shortly, but I rather imagine that about now you're pretty curious about what happened," Chris said. "Amy, why don't you do the honors?"

Amy spent the next several minutes giving Liz the high points of the afternoon, finishing with a thank you for Liz's meetings earlier with Maisie and Cody Merritt. "Without the input from them, I'm not sure we'd be raising a glass about now. Thank you."

"Not a problem. I'm glad I could do it. It looks like there will definitely be some changes happening at the spa," Liz said.

"Yes, and Zoe and I will get started on them tomorrow. But tonight, we celebrate. As a matter of fact, I think we all should go to the restaurant in the hotel for dinner. When Finn gets here, we'll see if he can join us."

A few minutes later, the front door opened and Zoe walked in. Amy and Chris ran to her, hugging her, and telling her how sorry they were she'd had to go through such an awful experience. Then Amy put her arm around Zoe and approached Liz.

"Zoe this is Liz, your biological mother. After you were arrested, we didn't know what to do, so we called her. She and her friend, Kelly, came here immediately, and without them, you'd still be in jail."

Liz and Zoe looked at each other for a long moment and then Zoe walked over to Liz and hugged her. "Thank you for everything. For giving me to these two wonderful people and helping me when I really needed some help."

At that Liz, Kelly, Chris, and Amy all had tears rolling down their cheeks, as did Zoe. Even Finn's eyes were unnaturally shiny. Chris was the first to speak, "Finn, we're going to the hotel restaurant for dinner tonight. I hope you can join us."

"I'd love to," he said, smiling at Zoe who smiled back.

"Wait, I have a question before I go in and shower and change clothes," Zoe said. "Kelly, when we first met, Finn introduced you as his associate. Does that mean you don't work for Finn?"

"It sure does. Finn and I met in the reception area at the jail. My son is an Oregon State Senator and when we found out about all of this, my husband called my son, who pulled some strings. Anyway, he was told that Finn O'Conner would be your public defender, because he was the best one around. Is that about it, Finn?" Kelly asked.

"Pretty much," Finn said. "I don't know about being the best one around, but I got a call that I would be handling this case and that my other cases were being given to some of the other attorneys in the office. Guess it helps to know people in high places."

"Guess it does," Zoe said. "Well, for whatever reason, I'm so glad all of you were able to help me. Thank you again."

"One thing, Liz, Kelly. I'd like you to stay tomorrow and just spend a day relaxing at the spa," Amy said. "I'll make facial and massage appointments for you, and you can go back home Monday instead of tomorrow. Would that work for you?"

"I originally told Kelly that I'd like to treat her to a weekend at a spa. I had no idea we really would do it," Liz said. "I think we could both use some down time. Thank you."

When Liz and Kelly got back to their suite following dinner, they decided it had to have been one of the best nights of their lives.

"Seriously Kelly, getting to meet my daughter and see what a wonderful young woman she has become was one of the high points of my life," Liz said.

"Well, one of the highlights of my life, although nothing as earth-shattering as yours, was that halibut and the carrots we had for dinner. I definitely have to figure out how to cook those. They were fabulous! And back to Zoe. Do you think you'll stay in touch with her?"

"I do. The awkward part of meeting each other is over, so I would think that, as long as I'm not intrusive, we should be able to maintain a very good relationship. I'm very thankful that Chris and Amy are so supportive of me."

"As well they should be, Liz. You dropped everything to come here and help them and ultimately, were very instrumental in Zoe's release from jail," Kelly said.

"And so were you. I'm looking forward to our spa treatments tomorrow and a long leisurely relaxing day. I called Doc and told him everything that had happened, and as usual, he was totally supportive and really happy for me."

"Liz, I want to run something by you and I want an honest answer from you. I talked to Amy before you got there tonight and she told me that Zoe had always said how much she'd love to meet her birth parents. Amy mentioned there was no way to get in touch with her birth father, but if there was, she knew Zoe would want to meet him."

"Why do I think I know where this is going?" Liz asked.

"Because you do. I'm going to the courthouse Monday and see if I can talk to Judge Murphy about Zoe. He may not want anything to do with her, but if he does, maybe I can arrange for Zoe to meet him. What do you think?"

"I think that would be great, but to be honest, I don't want to see him. Maybe that makes me a terrible person or something, but some of the most painful moments in my life are from my time with him and when I delivered Zoe with no family or friends to help me. I healed a lot by meeting Zoe, but I think that's the extent of how far I want to go."

"I understand completely. Do you mind if I go ahead with it?" Kelly asked.

"Not at all. You're going to do this Monday?"

"Yes. I remember that Zoe was going to be arraigned on Monday, so I'm assuming he'll be in his courtroom. Anyway, I thought I'd give it a try, and if it doesn't happen, well, it just wasn't meant to be."

"Obviously, you'll let me know what happens. It's been a really long day, and I'm wiped out. I'm off to bed. See you in the morning."

"Good night, dear friend. I'm so glad it all worked out with Zoe."

"Me, too," Liz said as she walked down the hall.

CHAPTER TWENTY-THREE

Kelly woke up Monday morning feeling refreshed after her day at the spa. She was sure Mike would notice her glowing cheeks from the facial and how smooth her body was after the long, wonderful massage. For the first time in a long time, she didn't feel any tension in her neck and made a mental note to schedule massages when she got back to Cedar Bay.

She and Liz had a leisurely breakfast and then they packed, so when Kelly returned from the courthouse, they'd be ready to head home. At 11:00 Kelly said, "Okay, I'm off. Wish me luck. I have no idea how this is going to turn out."

"Kelly, I'd put my money on you. I think you have a little angel over your head whose sole purpose in being is to make sure you're taken care of."

"I wish," she said as she opened the door of the suite. Ten minutes later she pulled into the county courthouse parking lot and looked up at the courthouse. She took a deep breath, got out of the car, and walked up the courthouse steps.

When she was inside, she looked at the roster of offices and saw that Judge Ryan's courtroom was in room number 3. She walked in that direction and saw that the doors were closed. She assumed he was in session and decided to sit and see what happened, assuming that there would be a lunch break.

A few minutes later, the doors to the court opened and several people came out. Kelly got up and walked into the courtroom. She saw a red-haired man in black robes sitting on the elevated bench in the front of the courtroom, who she assumed he was Ryan Murphy.

The room had completely cleared out and only Kelly and the judge were in it. She walked down the aisle between the chairs to where he was sitting. He looked up, saw her, and said, "May I help you?"

"Yes, Your Honor. My name is Kelly Reynolds. I have a personal matter to talk to you about. I'm a friend of Finn O'Conner's. If you're hesitant to talk to me, he can vouch for me."

"No, that won't be necessary," Judge Ryan said. "I'm a pretty good judge of character. Actually as a judge, I've learned to be a very good judge of character, and I don't think there will be a problem. What is this about?"

"Your Honor, I'd feel a lot more comfortable if we could go into your chambers. This really isn't something I want other people to hear."

Judge Murphy took a long look at her, and she could see

the resemblance to Zoe in the eyes and the mouth, to say nothing of the red hair. "Alright, this is highly unusual, but follow me." He stood up and walked over to a door which led to his chambers. "Please, have a seat and tell me what this is all about."

"Judge, many years ago you had a relationship with a woman named Liz. I don't know her maiden name. She became pregnant, and as I understand it, the timing was not good, since you were both in graduate school. I understand that you wanted to keep in touch with her, but she felt it was better to sever the relationship, and she did so before the baby was born."

Kelly could tell that the judge was listening to every word. A myriad of emotions crossed his face as she continued. "Liz chose to have the baby and give it up for adoption. She never told her family, because, as I understand it, they were very religious and would have probably disowned her."

Kelly paused and said, "Would you mind if I poured myself a glass of the water I see on the credenza?"

"Of course not," Judge Ryan said.

Kelly sat back down and continued. "A family member of Liz's was an attorney. He arranged for a private adoption and never told her parents. The adoptive parents were a young couple who were thrilled to be able to have a baby daughter."

"So the baby was a girl?" Judge Ryan asked. "I've often wondered."

"Yes, Your Honor. I'll make a long story short. You were to hold an arraignment this morning for a young woman accused of murdering Tina Lindsay, an employee at the Hillside Spa. That woman is your daughter, Zoe."

"Are you sure of this, Mrs. Reynolds?"

"Absolutely. I discovered that you were the father when I met with Zoe and her public defender, Finn O'Conner. In passing, he happened to mention that the judge who would be arraigning Zoe had red hair. Liz is my closest friend, and I began to put two and two together."

"I'm sorry, Mrs. Reynolds, but why would you be meeting with Finn and Zoe?"

She told him about the phone call from the Jannettes and what had led up to that meeting. "After I talked to Finn, I asked Liz some questions about Zoe's father. You see, Liz had never met Zoe, and didn't want their first meeting to take place in jail.

"Anyway, from what Liz told me I became convinced that you are her father. I asked Liz to do a computer background check on you to make sure your background information was what she knew of you and that the age was right. Everything matched up.

"I came here to Rolling Hills Crossing as a favor to Liz to see if I could help find out who the real murderer was. After finding out you were her father, I realized there was no way you could conduct a trial of your own daughter, even though it would be unbeknownst to you. When you found out, I imagined it would haunt you for the rest of your life. I made a vow to do everything I could to quickly find and identify the person who had committed the murder."

"I assume you were successful since I found out this morning when I came to my office that the charges had been dropped against Zoe and someone else had been charged with the murder," Judge Ryan said.

"That's correct, but that's not why I'm here. Liz and Zoe spent yesterday evening together and Zoe was thrilled to finally be able to meet her biological mother. She'd mentioned many times that she would like to meet her birth parents. She wanted to thank them for giving her up so the Jannettes could adopt her."

"And you're here because you think I should meet my daughter," the judge said.

"I'm not telling you that you should meet her, I'm simply telling you that you have a wonderful daughter who would be very open to having a relationship with you, but that's entirely your decision. Zoe and the Jannettes do not know that I'm here."

"To say I'm in a state of shock would be an understatement. Almost every day for the last twenty-four years I've thought about that child, and I've also wondered how Liz is."

"Liz is doing very well. She's a highly respected psychologist in Cedar Bay and married to a doctor, who adores her. She stayed in touch with the Jannettes and they would send her things about Zoe from time to time. That's how they happened to call Liz.

"They knew her husband was a doctor and might know people who could help Zoe. My son is a state Senator, and he was able to pull some strings and purportedly get the best public defender in the area."

"I wondered why Finn's schedule had been changed. That explains it." He took a deep breath. "Mrs. Reynolds, I'm happily married and have been for over twenty years, but unfortunately my wife and I were never able to have children. We thought about adopting, but I couldn't do it. I did tell her about fathering a child with Liz. Yes, I would like to meet Zoe, and I'm sure my wife would as well. Should I call or what?"

"Judge, why don't you let me do it? I think it would be too much of a shock for everyone to have you just show up. I'll talk to the Jannettes and see how they want to handle it. If you give me your number, I'll get back to you as soon as I talk to them."

"Here it is, Mrs. Reynolds. Let me write my cell phone number below the other number. I'll be waiting for your call. I never expected when I got here this morning to have my life turned upside down. I don't know if I should thank you or damn you," he said with a smile.

"I'd prefer a thanks," Kelly said, returning his smile.

Kelly walked out to her car, called Amy, and told her what had happened. Zoe was taking a break from the spa and was having lunch with her. Amy told Kelly she'd call her back after she'd discussed it with Amy.

Ten minutes later the Bluetooth in Kelly's car indicated an incoming call. It was Amy. "We've discussed it, including Chris, and we'd like Judge Murphy and his wife to come to dinner tomorrow night, say at 6:00. Should I call him, or will you?"

"I will," Kelly said with a smile, feeling that her time at the Hillside Resort had turned out to be one of the most inspirational moments of her life. She couldn't wait to tell Mike and Liz what had happened. The words "Truth is stranger than fiction" kept running through her mind."

EPILOGUE – SIX MONTHS LATER

"Hi guys," Kelly said as Liz and Doc walked into the coffee shop, grinning broadly. "You both look like the cat that ate the canary or whatever that saying is."

"Could be," Liz said. "When you have a minute, we'd like to talk to you."

"Be there in a few. You know where your booth is. Roxie's made sure that no one else took it. By the way, Charlie has a carrot dish as a special today that is fab. Good enough that even if someone didn't like carrots, they'd become fans. Might want to try it."

"That's a good enough recommendation for me. I'll give my order to Roxie," Doc said.

Kelly glanced over at them several times as she served orders and talked to customers. She could see them both smiling when they ate the carrots. She made a mental note to tell Charlie.

Finally, the rush of customers slowed down enough that Kelly was able to sit down at their booth. "Okay, my friends. What are you both so happy about?"

"Zoe called me last night, and you won't believe it, well, actually you might," Liz said.

"Liz, just get to the point. What did she have to say?"

"Well, remember how you kind of thought something might develop in Finn and Zoe's relationship?"

"Yes, I did."

"You were one hundred percent right. They're getting married in three months."

"Oh, Liz, that's wonderful. I really liked him. I am so happy for them."

"That's not even the best part," Doc said. "Wait till you hear this."

"I'm all ears."

"Well, you know that Ryan and Zoe have been seeing each other," Liz said.

"Yes, you've mentioned that they'd developed a very good relationship," Kelly said.

"Well, Chris is going to give Zoe away, as he should, but here's the best part. Ryan and his wife, Doc and me, and you and Mike, are all invited to the wedding and will be seated with the Janette's. Isn't that the best?" Liz said, clearly beside herself with joy.

"That absolutely is the best, and of course Mike and I will be there."

"And there's more. A jury found Raquelle guilty of murder and attempted murder. She's been sentenced to life in prison. And I'm starting to sound like some ad on television that keeps saying there's more, but there is."

"And that is?"

"Brett Lindsay wrote a letter to the judge from Mexico. Evidently, he's living there. In it he said he had not been involved in the death of his wife, but that Raquelle had confessed to him that she had murdered Tina because Tina wanted a larger share of the funds Raquelle was embezzling.

"That's why she was murdered. You know the sheriff tried to find Tina's account with the funds in it that she'd embezzled, but the account had been closed. He got a court order and it was determined that her husband had forged her name and gotten the funds. I imagine that's what he's living on in Mexico. From what Amy told me, he never returned to the hardware store, he just took off. Anyway, I couldn't wait to tell you everything."

"Well, Doc, who would have thought when you interrupted the call from Chris Jannette to tell him about me that all of this would have happened? So many lives changed because of just one thing. Utterly amazing."

"Keep your eye on the mail, because you should be receiving an invite in the next few weeks. This is so exciting. I think we need to go shopping in Portland. I really don't have a thing to wear," Liz said.

"I could say we could make it a weekend, but look what happened the last time we went away for a weekend," Kelly said with a laugh.

"I'm going to intercede here," Doc said. "A day trip, only a day trip."

RECIPES

BAKED BONELESS PORK CHOPS

Ingredients:
4 boneless pork chops
1 tbsp. olive oil
1 ½ tbsp. brown sugar
2 tsp. paprika
1 tsp. onion powder
1 tsp. dried thyme
1 tsp. salt
½ tsp. black pepper

Directions:
Preheat oven to 425 degrees. Line a rimmed baking sheet with parchment paper. Pat pork chops with paper towels. Rub pork chops with olive oil and place on prepared baking sheet. Combine brown sugar, paprika, onion powder, dried thyme, salt, and pepper in a small bowl and stir well to mix. Rub the spice mixture over all sides of the pork chops.

Bake for 15-20 minutes for 1-inch thick pork chop or

until internal temperature measures 145 degrees. (Thinner pork chops will cook faster and bone-in chops will take longer to cook. Don't overcook or they will become dry and tough.)

Remove from oven and let rest 5 minutes. Serve and enjoy!

IRON SKILLET APPLE PIE

Ingredients:
½ cup butter
1 cup brown sugar
1 pkg. refrigerated, rolled, unbaked pie crusts (I like to use Marie Callender pie crusts, 2 to a pkg.)
5 Granny Smith apples, peeled, cored, and sliced
¼ cup spiced rum (I like Captain Morgan Spiced Rum)
½ cup sugar
2 tsp. cinnamon
2 tsp. flour
1 egg + 1 tsp. water for egg wash, beaten together

Directions:
Preheat oven to 350 degrees. Put butter in a large, well-seasoned cast iron skillet. Transfer skillet to oven until butter is melted, about 5 minutes. Stir in brown sugar, return skillet to oven, and bake until bubbly, about 5 minutes more.

Carefully lay 1 pie crust on top of butter mixture. Arrange apple slices on top and drizzle with spiced rum. Stir sugar, cinnamon, and flour together in a small bowl.

Sprinkle mixture over apples. Lay remaining pie crust on top of the apples, making a few slits in it so steam can be release as it bakes.

Tuck top crust down to meet bottom crust along skillet sides. Brush top with beaten egg/water mixture. Bake until crust is golden brown and apples are tender, about 45-50 minutes.

Allow pie to cool until just warm, then serve topped with vanilla ice cream or whipped cream spiked with 2 tbsp. of spiced rum. Enjoy!

BROWN SUGAR GLAZED CARROTS

Ingredients:
1 lb. baby carrots (OK to use 4 regular size, roughly chopped)
2 tbsp. butter
1/3 cup brown sugar
1 cup water
Salt and pepper to taste

Directions:
In a medium saucepan, combine carrots with remaining ingredients and stir to blend. Bring to a boil over high heat. Reduce heat to medium and continue to softly boil (uncovered) for about 30 minutes, or until carrots are tender and the liquid has evaporated. Caution: Don't let brown sugar caramelize, keep soft glaze. Serve and enjoy!

NOTE: These are super-easy to make and so good!

SKILLET CHICKEN FAJITAS

Ingredients:
2 tsp. chili powder
½ tsp. ground cumin
¼ tsp. granulated garlic or garlic powder
3 boneless, skinless chicken breasts
¼ cup vegetable oil, divided
1 red bell pepper, seeded and sliced, julienne style
1 large onion, sliced
1 tbsp. lime juice
8 flour tortillas, warmed for serving
1 pkg. taco sauce made according to directions

Optional for serving:
shredded cheese, sliced jalapenos, cilantro, sour cream, guacamole, salsa, lime slices, chopped tomatoes

Directions:
In a large ziplock bag, combine the chili powder, cumin, and garlic. Add 2 tbsp. vegetable oil to the bag and mix to combine. Add the chicken breasts to the marinade while preparing the vegetables.

Heat a large cast iron or nonstick skillet over medium-high heat. Add 1 tbsp. vegetable oil and heat until shimmering. Add chicken breasts and cook for 4-5 minutes, or until seared on one side. Turn the chicken over and continue cooking until browned, about 5 minutes more. Remove the chicken, slice, and put in a warm oven.

Add 1 tbsp. vegetable oil to the skillet and heat. Add vegetables and cook, stirring occasionally, until the vegetables are soft and just beginning to brown. Add the sliced chicken and the taco mix. Cook until warm. Stir in lime juice and serve with warm tortillas. Enjoy!

CHOCOLATE CITRUS CAKE WITH GANACHE GLAZE

Ingredients:
¼ cup unsalted butter, room temperature, plus extra for greasing pan
1 cup flour, plus extra for pan
¼ cup cocoa powder
¾ tsp. baking soda
½ tsp. sea salt
3 oz. bittersweet chocolate, preferably 70%, finely chopped
1 ¼ cups light or dark brown sugar
2 large oranges, rinds finely grated (I use a microplane for this.)
2 tbsp. orange or lemon liqueur, such as Grand Marnier, Cointreau or Limoncello
2 extra large eggs, room temperature
1 cup strong brewed coffee, room temperature

Glaze:
2 oz. bittersweet chocolate, preferably 70%, finely chopped
1 tbsp. unsalted butter

Directions:
Preheat oven to 350 degrees. Grease the inside of a 9-inch round cake pan with butter and then line the bottom with a round of parchment paper. Grease the paper and

dust the inside of the pan with flour. Tap out the excess.

Sift flour, cocoa powder, baking soda, and salt into a medium bowl and whisk to combine. Place chocolate in a small bowl and microwave.

In a standing mixer bowl, combine the butter and brown sugar. Add the grated oranges and the liqueur. Beat on low speed until mixture is uniform. Increase speed to medium for approximately 4 minutes, or until light and fluffy. Add the eggs, one at a time, beating after each one. Add the melted chocolate and beat on low speed until combine. Add half of the coffee and half of dry ingredients. Beat and repeat until combined.

Pour batter into prepared pan and smooth the top. Bake until a toothpick inserted in the center comes out clean, approximately 40 – 45 minutes. Let cool completely in pan.

Ganache Glaze:
Place chocolate in small bowl. Juice one of the oranges and place ¼ cup in small saucepan. Put on high, and reduce until you have 3 tbsp. orange juice. Pour boiling hot juice over chocolate and gently mix with a small whisk. Add softened butter and whisk until combined, creating the ganache.

Invert the cake onto a rack and remove the pan and parchment paper. Invert again and plate. Spoon the ganache onto the top of the cake and using an offset spatula, gently spread it over the top. Serve and enjoy!

Note: Cake can be stored in an airtight container at room temperature up to one week.

LEAVE A REVIEW

I'd really appreciate it if you would take a few minutes and leave a review for Murder at the Spa.

Just go to the link below. Thank you so much. It means a lot to me ~ Dianne

Link: http://getbook.at/MATS

Paperbacks & Ebooks for FREE

Go to www.dianneharman.com/freepaperback.html and get your FREE copies of Dianne's books and favorite recipes immediately by signing up for her newsletter.

Once you've signed up for her newsletter you're eligible to win three paperbacks. One lucky winner is picked every week. Hurry before the offer ends!

ABOUT THE AUTHOR

Dianne lives in Huntington Beach, California, with her husband, Tom, a former California State Senator, and her boxer dog, Kelly. Her passions are cooking, reading, and dogs, so whenever she has a little free time, you can either find her in the kitchen, playing with Kelly in the back yard, or curled up with the latest book she's reading. Her award winning books include:

Cedar Bay Cozy Mystery Series

Cedar Bay Cozy Mystery Series - Boxed Set

Liz Lucas Cozy Mystery Series

Liz Lucas Cozy Mystery Series - Boxed Set

High Desert Cozy Mystery Series

High Desert Cozy Mystery Series - Boxed Set

Northwest Cozy Mystery Series

Northwest Cozy Mystery Series - Boxed Set

Midwest Cozy Mystery Series

Midwest Cozy Mystery Series - Boxed Set

Cottonwood Springs Cozy Mysteries

Cottonwood Springs Cozy Mysteries - Boxed Set

Midlife Journey Series

Midlife Journey Series - Boxed Set

The Holly Lewis Mystery Series

Holly Lewis Mystery Series - Boxed Set

Miranda Riley Paranormal Cozy Mystery Series

Chef Dani Rosetti Cozy Mystery Series

Maria Rodriguez Mystery Series

Debut Cozy Mystery Series

A Cozy Cookbook Series

Coyote Series

Red Zero Series

Black Dot Series

Audiobooks
Her audiobooks can be found at
http://dianneharman.com/audiobooks.html

Newsletter
If you would like to be notified of her latest releases please go to www.dianneharman.com and sign up for her newsletter.

Website: www.dianneharman.com,
Blog: www.dianneharman.com/blog
Email: dianne@dianneharman.com

COMING SOON

PUBLISHING 5/29/21

MURDER IN NEW MEXICO– BOOK 15

COTTONWOOD SPRINGS COZY MYSTERY SERIES

http://getbook.at/MNM

Cold case murder investigations are a lot harder to solve than current murder cases.

Particularly when the murder occurred over fifteen years ago.

But when a friend asks Brigid to investigate a cold case for her in New Mexico,

Brigid feels she has to at least try.

What she hadn't taken into consideration

Were old grudges,

A small town that kept secrets,

And people who were willing to commit hate crimes to keep those secrets.

Join Brigid and Jett, her 125-pound Newfoundland dog, as they try to find the long-ago killer. But not so long ago that the threat of her discovering the identity of the killer makes her a present-day target.

Dogs, recipes, and page-turning action all come together in Murder in New Mexico, the 15th book in the Cottonwood Springs Cozy Mystery Series by a USA Today Bestselling Author.

Printed in Great Britain
by Amazon

82630519R00102